CALL THESE STORIES

by

Dick Wild

Grosvenor House
Publishing Limited

This book is published by
Grosvenor House Publishing Ltd
28-30 High Street, Guildford, Surrey, GU1 3EL.
www.grosvenorhousepublishing.co.uk

A CIP record for this book
is available from the British Library

ISBN 978-1-78148-803-4

Foreword......

As ever, my aim is to write short stories, as in the *real* sense of the word...short!.. that are varied in ideas, settings and styles, and are immediately accessible to the reader. If you enjoy reading *some*, if not *all* the stories, thank you for taking the time and trouble. If you don't like any of them, thanks for giving it a go!

In either case, you may like to try my previous collections.. '14 Shorts...' and 'Sweet & Sour'...pretty much more of the same, you may (or may not) be pleased to hear!

Contents

The Shootist

Alistair De-Lane stood staring out of the window. It was one of those bedraggled, misty afternoons, like looking out on a wet graveyard in the middle of February.

He reached down and opened the third drawer, shuffling shirts and odd socks aside until his fingers closed on the catapult's metal handle. He closed the drawer. His mother would be occupied downstairs – making tea probably. And his father wouldn't be back from work for a while yet.

He turned the catapult repeatedly in his fingers. There was little to compare with the feel of a proper catapult, the sheer simplicity: the firm metal stem that slotted neatly in the palm, the rubber – loose now, yet taut and tough as gristle when retracted. There had been a number of risks in obtaining it – but that was the point; that was what made it the *real thing*: like waiting for the right man serving behind the counter at the fishing-and-guns shop in town, and coming to terms with the fact that it was going to take care of several weeks pocket-money.

He reached for the lead-pellet tin, taking one of the ball-bearings – the heavy ones this time, the real bulbous ones, about the size of pigeon-eggs, that he had got from the toy shop next door in town – slotting it into the small leather pouch. Fortunately the window opened on the right, enabling him to aim beyond the line of fences without having to open it to its full width.

With the ball-bearing weighing to a point just an inch or so beneath his chin, he tried gauging the whereabouts of the greenhouse, clear enough in his mind's eye yet several gardens away and – as importantly, in light of the mist – entirely out of vision.

Bracing himself against the window-sill, and with his eye on the flat expanse of distant trees, he made a quick adjustment to the angle, and with the customary stir of anticipation, released the steel-bearing – able, at first, to follow its tracer-bullet trajectory, before swiftly withdrawing from sight, backing himself against the curtain, in readiness for the distant tinkle of glass, that, as ever, failed to materialise.

It was a familiar story; however many times he tried, for some reason it never seemed to happen – frustrating, considering each ball-bearing being wasted, and particularly the bigger ones that didn't come cheap. He'd tried just about every conceivable angle – over the trees, through the trees, round the trees! – he might just as well have been firing at the far side of the moon.

Bracing himself against the curtain, and resolved, as ever, to give it another go, he turned again to the window, this time in the other direction.

Opening it to its full width and turning to his right, he took a second weight from the box and reloaded the pouch, levelling the catapult at – again – what he calculated to be just about the right angle, his eye hovering somewhere beneath the angled rooftops.

Grimacing at the feel of the elastic stretched to a point just beneath his right cheek – he steadied the V and unleashed the steel ball – again able to follow its initial jettison, this time into a no-man's land of garden sheds and shrubbery beyond a line of trellis-fencing, before quickly backing himself up against the curtain to await the inevitable stony-silence.

Once again he shrugged it off. Fortunately it wasn't, and never had been, simply a matter of hitting (or in his case – missing) a target, or there'd have been little point from the start. It was something more than that; some hangover from his upbringing perhaps – days spent alone in his playpen banging a toy rattle aimlessly against the bars. Or before that: chasing bison up and down hills with sharpened sticks and handfuls of stones.

In his case, certainly something picked up on during his junior years – an obsession with hand-held weapons: bows-and-arrows, pea-shooters, spud-gun, catapults – their simplicity being key: small and neat, slotting snugly in the palm of his hand.

He looked again at the metal V and strands of elastic hanging from it….a *proper* catapult – not the pathetic home-made jobs – a couple of clothes pegs tied together with a floppy rubber band that invariably split and just about managed to plop the stone about thirty yards up the street…The *real* thing – factory-made, the metal gleaming – the rubber taut and firm, pulled tight as a tendon to a point just under your chin – straining for its moment of release. And – knowing there was always the next time: that next time he might, quite literally, strike lucky. And it was hardly his fault if people were in the habit of constantly shifting their greenhouses.

It was as he was re-loading the pouch, contemplating one more go at the greenhouse on the left, that he was aware of a rustling noise much closer to home; something stirring in the bushes in the neighbouring garden. He peered into the gloom. Maybe a bird, or a cat foraging around for something in a bush. Then another rustle – a bunch of leaves shuddering violently and then drifting apart before dropping mysteriously back into place. He watched – intrigued. It seemed strange in the midst of such deathly hush.

Almost in passing, he raised the stem, drew the elastic and promptly released the ball bearing in the direction of the errant bush, able this time to follow its more immediate trajectory, and – seconds later – a moment of frenzy as the bushes appeared to go into some kind of overdrive, leaves thrashing about in all directions, before finally stirring and coming to settle – back to a state of near-stillness.

He gave it a moment and then pulled the window shut and was in the process of replacing the catapult under a shirt and pullover in the third drawer down when he heard a voice.

'Alistair!' It was his mother. It was *always* his mother.

He looked at his watch. He'd best go down or she might come up looking for him. He closed the drawer and prepared to make an appearance.

'Oh there you are.'

She was waiting at the bottom of the stairs.

'I was wondering what had happened to you,' she said, her eyelashes flickering in the hall-light.

'I was upstairs,' he said.

'I know,' she said. 'I know you were upstairs. Now – go and get you planner...'

She turned to the kitchen.

Alistair turned to his school bag.

He returned to find her standing there, armed with a pen.

'Okay – let me see it.'

The planner was a kind of diary issued by the school to record homework details and other items worthy of note; effectively a two-way communication between home and school. Each double side covered a week and each week the planner would be signed and a comment added, if desired, in the space provided.

Alistair's mother always made a point of adding a comment as well as signing the page. It took very little time and she saw it as one of her duties as a caring parent. For most of the kids the planner was little more than an opportunity for a little off-the-cuff graffiti: girlfriend's or boyfriend's names – penned in jagged highlighter: initials carved in mega-hearts and rainbow-coloured hoops and stars. All – a breach of school rules, but no-one seemed to notice, least of all, the parents – except in Alistair's case.

There would be little point in attempting to explain such things to his mother.

He waited patiently as she undertook a detailed examination of each immaculately uncluttered page: the H.E. teacher's request to bring the ingredients for making scones next Tuesday, the form-teacher's reminder that the following Thursday would be an Inset-Day for the teachers, signing the square himself as evidence. She leant to write something, adding her initials underneath.

She looked up. She had come across two coloured stars: one on Tuesday's page, one on Wednesday's – the first for English, the second for P.H.S.E.

'Good boy,' she said. 'Did you add them to your total?' She turned to the back, to a page consisting of columns of squares designed to be filled in with each newly acquired merit.

'Good. That's excellent. Your father will be pleased. Forty-six merits so far. That's good.'

'It depends on the teachers,' said Alistair quickly, watching as she wrote...*I am delighted that Alistair achieved two merits this week. Well done Alistair!* in the appropriate space.

She returned to the previous page.

'Good...Okay...Homework after tea...And it's 'Thursday Tigers' tonight. Do you need to take anything?' He shook his head.

'Are you sure?'

He shook his head again.

'Right...Okay...Good.'

He took the planner and went to replace it in his bag. She looked up, making her way back to the kitchen.

'Here's your father. Show him the two stars.'

He looked up to see the car's headlamps drift into the hallway and kitchen. Moments later a car-door slammed and the kitchen door opened. His father stepped across to kiss his wife on the cheek.

A few minutes later, having taken his bag back upstairs, Alistair seated himself on the far side of the table. His father followed shortly, taking his seat at the head of the table. Later, his mother entered carrying a dish...

'Cottage pie,' she announced, placing the dish on the table.

'Looks good,' said his father, leaning for a closer look. 'Fit for a king.' He looked at Alistair.

'The difference between shepherds pie and cottage pie...? The spoon hovered in readiness to reward the right answer.

'Cottage pie is minced beef,' said Alistair.

'Correct,' said his father, sinking the spoon into the layer of lightly glazed potato.

'Shepherds pie – lamb. Shepherds…lamb!' said his mother appearing through the doorway bearing a tray of vegetables – carrots and peas, and placing it in the centre of the table.

Tea commenced.

His father tapped the side of the plate with his knife.

'This is good,' he said. His mother reached across to spoon a small portion of carrots and peas onto her plate. 'Cost you five pounds in a café,' said his father, looking at Alistair and tapping the side of the plate with a spoon.

'And Alistair's been good at school,' she said, her voice rising in time with the spooning of each of the two vegetables. 'He got two merits this week! He was going to show you.'

'Good,' said his father. 'For…?'

'English…And we're not sure what the other one was for are we?' said his mother, spooning a few peas on the side of her plate.

'P.H.S.E,' said Alistair.

'That's right – English and P.H.S.E,' said his mother.

'Good…Well done Alistair,' said his father.

'Yes – well done Alistair…And well done the teachers,' said his mother.

'Yes – Well done everyone,' said his father, spooning an extra portion of cottage pie on his plate now it had done the rounds, and adding a few more peas. 'Every little helps,' he said, 'with SATs in two years.'

'Yes – and you watch the two years fly by,' added his mother, forking a small amount of pie in readiness to raise it to her mouth. 'It'll have gone before you know it,' she said.

'This is good,' said his father, tapping the plate and looking approvingly at his wife.

His mother tapped the dish. 'There's more if you want.' She was looking first at her husband and then at Alistair.

Alistair shook his head. He had enough on his plate already.

'We'll see,' said his father, loosening his tie with the exertion of eating. He'd already helped himself to a little extra.

'That was good,' said his father some time later, watching a steaming dish of apple-pie being carried into the room....

'Apple pie,' announced his father.

'With fresh cream,' added his mother, placing the dish in the centre of the table.

It was shortly after tea when Alistair was in his room popping the requirements for the following day in his school bag: planner, games-kit and reading book for English – that the doorbell rang.

There followed something of a commotion, the details of which would be difficult to recall, but it led to voices calling up the stairs and along the landing.

'Alistair...!' 'Alistair..!'

It was his mother and father. He'd best go down.

His parents were stood at the bottom of the stairs ashen-looking and seeming strangely distraught. Next to them was Mrs. Coleman, wife of an elderly couple next door, and behind her – her two sons. For a moment no-one spoke.

'Alistair!' repeated his mother, wearing an expression of incredulity.

Alistair looked to the ground and began to make his way down the stairs.

Night Hawks

A lone figure stood half-way down the street – two hands clamped in the pockets of his great-coat, head hunched deep into his collar, pulled high in semi-protection from the wearying drizzle that continued to skirt the night-lamps like swarms of tiny moths.

The part of the street where he was standing was in almost total shadow; the only light – a ferocious light behind a stretch of glass panelling some ten to twenty yards away but in clear view from where he was standing. In contrast to its surroundings of shuttered windows and empty doorways, the glass was dazzlingly clean and shimmering under the steady onslaught of drizzle. Behind the glass an array of furnishings stood like a tiny theatrical stage – a corner standard lamp, plastic sofa and an artificial tree perched at a perilous angle in a basin filled with tiny pebbles – all preserved under the glow of two ceiling-height fluorescent strips.

The man outside the building continued to observe the scene: a long pine-wood desk a good thirty to forty feet away from the door. Behind which, a man sat on a swivel chair reading a book.

He was a middle-aged, slightly balding man, with a heavy upper torso and slightly rounded shoulders. He was a few sizes too large for the chair upon which he was seated, prompting periodic shifts of his buttocks in an attempt to secure a more comfortable posture.

He occasionally looked up from his magazine, partly a matter of routine, but more particularly in the last few minutes, in response to what he had perceived to be some movement or interruption to his vision somewhere out in the street to the right of the window. He made little of it, resigned to it being little more than his imagination; not unusual in a lonely vigil such as his, stretching as it did, through the long hours of darkness, with little to divert it, except – on nights such as this – long looping rivulets of rain running in patterns down the panes of glass. With little more than a casual glance at the window, he returned to the next page of his book.

The man outside had taken a few steps nearer to the window, partly to evade the worst excesses of the drizzle and partly for a better view. He drew a cigarette from his pocket and lit it behind the protection of cradled fingers, hunching himself deeper into the coat lapels, his eye fixed firmly on the figure now solidly within his sights.

It was at the fifth or sixth hint of distraction, that the man put the book to one side, ventured over to the window and peered into the rain-swept street.

On the fringe of the hanging light and semi-obliterated by the strip-lighting from within the building – was the unmistakeable figure of a man, blurred in refractions of rain, yet clear enough to be seen looking in his direction. What he was doing in the street at this hour and peering into the foyer window was anybody's guess, though he appeared to be waiting for someone or something, deliberately positioned at the edge of the pavement to the side of the window.

The man felt obliged to open the door, if only to confirm he wasn't hurt or in some sort of trouble. He reached for the upper and lower bolts and taking a key from a belt at his waist, unlocked the door and eased it a few inches from the jamb. He could even now only vaguely make out the facial features a few yards away, dripping under the soaked hat.

'You okay?' he called, as much into the darkness of the street as to the figure lurking by the window. The man shrugged and brushed his hand against the onslaught of rain now battering relentlessly against his shoulders. The man in the office threw a quick glance up the length of the street and held the door open a little further.

'You want to come in for a moment. Get a bit of shelter?' he asked, holding the door at the narrowest of angles.

The man muttered curt gratitude and stepped into the frame, smacking his feet against the mat.

After the rain-swept chill of the street, the foyer entrance area was warm and welcoming, like the entrance to some large, swanky hotel. The walls by the window were huge cream-scaped panels adorned with heavy splashes of modern art-work: a mish-mash of vague shapes and colours, jig-sawed around wailing expressions and horrifically distorted faces. The settee and lamp stood comfortably in the far-corner recess, giving way to a large carpeted open-plan reception area flanked by the pine-wood desk and a couple of doors and grey filing cabinets to one side.

The man stood a moment observing the scope of décor and furnishings and then brushed an excess of rain from the folds of his sleeve. Apart from the two of them, there was no sign of life – almost as if the building had been air-lifted by night onto some deserted plateau on the surface of the moon.

The first man had resumed his position behind the desk. Only when seated, did he turn to his visitor – still heavily coated, the lapels pulled high – brushing himself down against the evening's worst excesses.

'Terrible night,' he said.

'Mmm....Just got worse.' He looked up, seeking to take advantage of a new perspective on the surroundings.

'It's the office of a Company,' said the first man, sensing an air of curiosity. 'Finance Company – dealing in and offering a range of services.'

He stopped, his fingers tapping lightly on the surface of the desk, studying his visitor for any sign of approval. 'Short and long-term collateral. Hedge-funding. Asset-stripping. Providing collateral for an international Banking Group. I'm not at liberty to reveal any further details.'

Either it failed to register or the guy simply wasn't that interested. He had stepped across the foyer to steps leading to a deeper, darker area away from the entrance doors. The man watched him halt just before the steps, his eye venturing to the area beyond, referred to in-house as the 'inner-sanctum'.

'The office areas are up a few flights of stairs to the left – four floors of them in fact.'

The man looked briefly, but displayed little intent of investigating further, which was just as well, as he would have had to quickly intervene – the 'inner-sanctum' being off-limits to all but employees of the Company. Instead, he turned, and looked back across the entrance area, at the deep hues of the carpet and the rain-spattered windows beyond.

'Quite a big place then,' he said, still patting the lingering strains of damp along his sleeve.

'Fairly.'

The man at the desk toyed with disclosing some details. He didn't often get visitors, maybe there wouldn't be any harm in offering a little explanation. He brushed the book to one side and rose from his chair.

'I'm the…Night Superintendent.' The words carried a sense of pride that might be reflected in a badge worn as confirmation of the fact.

'My name's Wood – John Wood,' said the visitor, still directing his attention to the rain-streaked window and the darkness of the street.

There was no offering of hands. For one thing there was still some distance between them, and secondly it seemed a little out of sorts considering the circumstances. Instead, he cocked an eye at a picture his guest had spotted above a cabinet to the left and moved in to offer a little explanation.

'Hopper…Cape Cod Morning,' he said, with a nod of approval. In the picture, a woman alone in a room was leaning towards a bay-window, peering out into what appeared to be an area of fields, flanked by a forest. The window was a huge frame of glass – almost dominating the frame.

He had his eye fixed on the woman's blank expression.

'See the way she's peering away from the house – toward the sensation of space.' He moved closer, indicating the area with his right index finger.

The man said nothing, leaving the Superintendent to ponder over the picture's hidden qualities – the thick bank of trees running the length of the frame.

'She looks bored,' he said, dismissing both window and woman and re-directing himself toward the centre of the foyer.

'Mmm...maybe she is,' said the Superintendent, his eye lingering a moment – searching for the object of the woman's gaze – possibly some disturbance in the depths of trees.

The visitor was back – standing directly under the arc of light.

'So you look after this place then.'

'That's right.'

'At night.'

'That's right...all night. Throughout the night.'

The Superintendent returned to his desk. The visitor watched his movements, trying to visualise how he may fare in the event of physical confrontation. For all the man's bulky physique, his movements were slow and he guessed he might struggle were someone to pull a few quick punches. He watched him resume his place behind the desk and reach for the book, which he held up to his guest's eye.

'Kafka......'The Castle',' he said, turning his eye on the blank, featureless cover. 'A land-surveyor arrives at a village to work at a castle. But, typically, as one might expect in Kafka's work, the place remains elusive, beyond access, to him or to anyone else it seems – at least ostensibly.' He looked wistfully at the cover and returned it to the desk.

Outside there seemed little likelihood of a cessation in the weather. The Superintendent lifted an eye from the page and looked towards the window.

'I was under the impression you were waiting for someone,' he said, turning to where his visitor had taken a perch on the arm of the plastic chair. 'I could just about make you out, out of the corner of my eye, standing in the rain.'

'I wasn't waiting for anyone,' he said, after a moments' thought. 'I'd just been out and I was trying to get out of the rain for a while and I saw the light. And then I noticed you sitting behind the desk.'

The Superintendent eased the book to one side. He often tired of reading by around this time and invariably found his mind wandering, his thoughts drifting towards the up and coming hours of early morning.

'Well John….You don't mind me using your name.' He raised a questioning eye. 'You can stay a while until the rain stops if you like…..If it stops.'

Their eyes turned simultaneously to the window – mutual acknowledgement that it seemed unlikely for some time yet.

The visitor shrugged and stepped a few feet across the carpet, taking in the wall space for any further points of interest.

'Thanks.'

In addition to the works of art and a mirror just above the plastic sofa, there were two clip-board displays of print with what looked like the name of the company embossed at the top. There was little to grab the eye, but someone had pinned them up intending them to be looked at. He started from the top.

'Just some of the conditions and codes of practice currently in force,' explained the Superintendent, aware still of his obligation to follow his visitor's every move.

The 'codes of practice' were quickly abandoned in favour of his former position perched on the plastic arm.

'So your job is to stay here all night and look after the place,' he said.

'That's right,' said the Superintendent – head resting on neatly folded arms – the pose of a man at one with his chosen lot in life. He extended an arm to the parameters of his domain: window, the cabinets, the stairs to the 'inner sanctum' and its office areas waiting beyond.

'All night – every night – three hundred and sixty five nights a year,' he said in a tone that was quick to dispel the idea this was some run-of-the-mill operation – some ten-a-penny venture to be found most anywhere in the city.

His visitor continued to scan the extent of his host's domain, whether from sympathy or a grudging sense of admiration, was difficult to gauge.

'All year round then – no break – no holidays.'

'Three hundred and sixty five days a year. No break. No time off.' confirmed the Superintendent. 'Whilst children open toys under the eyes of parents, and families make their annual pilgrimage to Midnight Mass, I'm sitting right here behind this desk.' He leant back, arms cradled: the pose of a man prepared to take some pride in such selfless levels of commitment.

His guest's eye drifted once more to the window, where the blurry contours and miniscule patterns had effectively obliterated any sign of the street.

'Don't you get bored?' he asked, trying to picture himself in a role that appeared so spectacularly undemanding.

The question, logical though it seemed, appeared to sink the Superintendent into an idle finger-tapping on the desk. He sighed, indication of his defences weakening a little.

'Yes…if I'm honest, I suppose I do get a little bored,' he said, prepared finally to concede that his chosen lot in life, didn't, at first glance, appear to have a great deal to commend it. He laid his arms across the pinewood desk in the manner of a teacher about to lay a few facts before an errant pupil.

'But so are most people's wouldn't you say? Wouldn't you say that most people's jobs are little more than the desultory passing of time?'

The visitor shrugged and looked across at the empty stairs.

'Maybe,' he said…. 'Maybe.'

The Superintendent had begun leafing through a stapled collection of sheets, occasionally ticking parts before turning to the next. The process came under temporary scrutiny of his visitor, until he turned his attention once more to the foyer, and a second picture pinned in the centre of the left hand wall, above a collection of plastic plants.

The Superintendent watched him make his way across the foyer to the picture, allowing time for an initial appraisal before placing the sheaves of paper on the desk to join the man, peering over his shoulder, his eye joining the images captured within the frame.

'Nighthawks.' The title was sufficient to sink the pair into a moment's silence. The scene was a corner diner somewhere in a US. city at night: its brightly lit interior a stark contrast to the street's almost eerie darkness. Inside the diner, a couple laze against the counter, half chatting to the owner, whilst across the bar, a single figure, a man, sits in isolation, seemingly lost in his private thoughts.

The Superintendent's eye followed the glare from the right-hand corner into the street. 'Note the use of light and space.' His hand mapped out a vague area to the left side of the print.

The visitor, whose eye had fixed on the rear part of the picture, leant closer and pointed a finger.

'There's a cash-till in the top window,' he said.

The Superintendent nodded. The till was placed close to a window on the left hand side of the frame. He looked back at the picture.

'So...the question is..*why* is it there? And....what about the man?....Is there a robbery pending?'

The Superintendent peered into the glass.

'Or maybe it's just three bored people sitting in a café at night,' he said.

It was as the Superintendent leant to consider the possibility that the man's attention was drawn again to the foyer, where the rain had taken to sweeping the glass in a dramatic upsurge of tempo.

'Getting worse,' said the visitor, crossing to the window to take a closer look at the street, suddenly awash in swirling torrents.

The Superintendent made his way back to his desk, taking the stapled sheets and hanging them on a hook to the left of the filing cabinet. To his right was a wooden compartment almost built into the wall. He rose from his chair and settled on his haunches to open the doors for a quick check on three dials placed side by side against the wooden panelling.

'Temperature gauges and security monitor,' he explained, looking up and across his shoulder. 'The needle should hover just between these two points indicated by two black markers.' His visitor looked again at his watch and across at the desk. The wall-cabinet check completed, the Superintendent closed the door and returned to his desk.

'So you have things to do then, to keep you busy.'

'I have certain duties to tend to, yes, certain procedures that need to be followed, matters that have to be sorted and checked.'

The visitor shifted in his seat, sensing that in light of the weather, and with strangers apparently waiting to drop in on him at the drop of a hat – he may be contemplating drawing the evening to a close. He looked again at his watch and stretched his legs in an exaggerated display of lethargy.

'Well I have to say this,' he said, slapping an arm against the chair and gazing out on the glazed reflections on the pavement. 'There aren't many who could do what you do – sit here night after night – nothing to look at, nothing to see. Nothing whatsoever to brighten up your evening and I have to say....I don't envy you.' He slapped a few more beats and fixed his eye on the stair that led the way to the 'inner sanctum' and whatever lay beyond.

'So...what exactly goes on up there? Anything worth seeing?'

The Superintendent shifted in his seat, partly to bring life back to his right buttock that seemed to have deadened itself from a lack of breathing space.

'That's the office area,' he said.

The man's curiosity was stirred – enough to tempt him a little further.

'Well, let's take a look,' he said. 'There must be something up there. Come on. We're both bored – there's nothing happening down here – it's pissing with rain – there must be something worth seeing beyond a few paintings and a plastic sofa....'

The Superintendent looked in the direction of the stairs and the 'inner sanctum' and then back to his visitor, whose eye hadn't strayed from his. He gave it a moment's thought and shifted again in his seat.

'Okay,' he said. 'As it happens, at this time of night I have to do a little tour of duty – a walkabout, you might call it – just to check that all's well. So, if you'd be interested, you'd be welcome to join me.'

The visitor remained seated for a moment, as if weighing the pros and cons of the offer before committing himself.

The pair rose from their chairs, The Superintendent wriggling to restore the feeling to his buttock and make a few quick adjustments to a keyboard panel. He turned a key behind a small door in the wall and went to check the main door and the bolts.

'Okay,' he said, making his way towards the stairs. 'Follow me.'

They made their way across the carpeted floor.

'This is mostly off-limits to visitors,' he reminded his guest, quick to point out the favour he was bestowing. The visitor followed, deliberately keeping some distance between them.

'This is the stairway that takes us to the main floors of the office,' said the Superintendent, waiting for him to draw level.

Together they made their way to a wide, carpeted stairwell and began to climb the stairs. It was a full four flights before they eventually arrived in a long room that was bare, save for a series of low coffee-type tables and a door at the end.

Lines of desks and computer screens ran the entire length of the room, whilst the far wall was a mass of grey filing cabinets. To its right, and stretching the full length of the right side of the office, was a huge plate-glass window, opening onto the night-time expanse of the City's buildings.

The men stood side by side, taking in the cluster of towers, rain-swept squares and abandoned pavements. The visitor made his way to the glass, stretching his eye down to street level, skirting left and right along the expanse of rain-washed rooftops and near-invisible side-streets.

'Impressive isn't it?' The Superintendent had placed himself a few feet behind to allow his guest full benefit of the spectacle beneath them.

'Mm, quite a view,' said the visitor. 'Pity about the rain.' He turned to make his way back to the central space of the office. 'Just one of the perks,' said the Superintendent, his eyes drawn to the patterns of light extending to its furthest and darkest corners...'rain or no rain.'

'What about that room there?' said the visitor, already making his way toward a door at the far end of the office.

The silence was taken as an open invitation. He looked briefly over his shoulder, waiting for the Superintendent to join him.

It was a tiny room, much darker, geared more to off-duty relaxation than the completion of business. At the rear of the room, a series of chairs backed away from a line of filing cabinets, whilst at the front, two swivel chairs stood aside a small coffee table. The room was in darkness, lifted just a fraction by a narrow eclipse of light from the hallway through the semi-open door. The dominant feature – as in the office next door – was a huge glass window opening onto the neighbouring streets, or in this case, a row of tenement buildings directly opposite.

The visitor made his way to the front, where he looked out across the street facing a line of grey washed-out buildings. And then he turned and made his way to the rear of the room, leaning close to the wall.

'So, what happens now?' he asked.

The Superintendent hesitated, looking first at his watch and then back at his visitor who had remained by the wall near the door.

The chain of thought was broken a movement towards the glass-panelled window.

'Just take a seat over there.' He indicated a line of chairs on the right side of the room. His visitor's eye drifted from the Superintendent to the window and the seats indicated beneath.

Each man was seated in pole-position just in front of the window: a far from unfamiliar scenario: two men alone in a tiny cinema – seated and waiting for the opening titles to roll.

It was about thirty seconds later that a window on the third floor of the tenement block opposite, was suddenly bathed in an orange glow. Seconds later, a figure emerged from the wings into the room to ease the curtains to one side and lean gently toward the glass, peering out into the night.

The figure was a woman; a youngish woman, maybe in her early thirties, with a mane of hair that flowed over her shoulders to halfway down her back. Seconds later, she took a few paces back into the full crescent of light at the centre of the room. And then, moving slowly and rhythmically in a close caressing dance with the air in front of her, she slipped the dress or smock from her shoulders. It flopped to the floor, revealing her nude body to the night sky and the office window pitched in darkness on the fourth floor of the block opposite, behind which, the Superintendent and his guest sat watching the scene in silence.

For some three to four minutes, the woman turned and pirouetted under the orange light-bulb, her hips drifting in and out of the light, her hands lowering and then rising along the flanks of her back to bunch her hair into a provocative pose, staring intently at the window, and the office block opposite. The men watched in silence – like two estranged relatives marking time before a family funeral. Only occasionally, did an eye turn on the Superintendent; checking for any sudden or untoward movements. But the Superintendent remained quite unperturbed, both arms placed firmly behind his head – clear indication of little beyond a little harmless voyeurism – as the woman continued to sway naked under the light.

A few closing pirouettes and leggy strides across the room, and she reached down for her gown which she raised to her shoulders, taking a quick glance at the building opposite; after which, she withdrew behind the curtains, which were promptly drawn to a close.

The Superintendent rose from his seat and without casting so much as an eye on his visitor, made his way to the door at the rear, where – still half-shadowed against the light from the hall, he stood, head bowed, waiting for his guest to leave the room so he could shut the door. It was quite likely that – in the heat of the moment – neither of them had noticed that the rain had dwindled to little more than a few spots.

Once back in the foyer, the Superintendent stood at the window, glancing out into the street. The rain had ceased, leaving its pools in gutters and its reflections of a newly broken moon across the buildings and rooftops.

'Rain's stopped,' he said, venturing an eye to the pavement sidelight where he had first spotted the man peering into his window. The visitor drew level, pulling his collar tight to his neck.

'Could still be a bit chilly mind.'

The Superintendent nodded and reached for the bolts of the door. It was the visitor who broke the silence.

'Quite a show,' he said.

There was no response from the Superintendent – just a nod as he released the upper catch and unlocked the door.

'Just one thing though....'

As he stepped from the comfort zone of the foyer into the windswept chill of the street, he turned to look again at the Superintendent, his hands hugging his pockets as protection against the cold.

'I'd be a little careful.'

The Superintendent stood at the door waiting to oversee his departure.

'I mean, you never know who else might be watching, could be her husband, or maybe her brother...you never know.'

He stepped onto the pavement and looked quickly back into the foyer light, before making his way down the street.

'Thanks for the shelter,' he said, looking over his shoulder one last time and disappearing under the fading lamp-light.

The Superintendent stood at the door, before reaching down to draw the bolts and complete the centre-lock. He stepped slowly across the illuminated space to his pinewood desk, reaching for his book, though he always found it difficult to concentrate on text at this time of night.

He looked toward the fringe of light hanging in the street, but there would be no further interruptions to his routine that night.

The Interview

The interviewee walked through the gates and into the small car parking area which had few, if any, remaining spaces to park in. The cars were the usual range: a few dubious run-of-the-mill affairs at one end, a few grander types for the more senior employees at the other end.

The building's façade comprised a series of dark blue prefab-style squares set into the tall blocks of small brick construction, awarding the whole complex, and particularly the central edifice, a general air of dishevelment and pre-fab sixties' shabbiness.

He followed the sign *All visitors please report to reception* which took him into a small entrance area with a worn green carpet and a glass windowed screen at the top end, behind which a number of women busied themselves on computers or at the shelves of drawers. Initially his presence went unnoticed, but eventually one of them saw fit to abandon her keyboard and approach the screen.

'Can I help you?' The voice seemed to waver, as if uncertain as to the credentials of the person it was addressing.

He explained his circumstances and the voice directed him to a corridor, up the stairs, left and then right and left again to a point he wasn't sure he'd remember, but wouldn't ask to be repeated for fear of appearing stupid; he could always ask again. He thanked her and she responded, of sorts, and returned to her screen.

He made his way along the corridor, half glancing at a few posters on road safety and 'The Route To Success At Key Stage Four', curled at its edges and just about clinging to existence by virtue of a few pieces of dry blue-tac. The background of noise, blurred behind walls and punctuated by the occasional shout of teacher or pupil, was audible the length of the corridor.

He continued up the stairs and eventually found the room: a small, carpeted computer room not far from the staffroom. A number of chairs had been arranged in a small circle and two people, presumably fellow candidates, had already occupied two of them. They sat, self-consciously cross-legged in their tidy pressed suits and acknowledged him with a brief raise of the hand and forced smiles.

Others duly arrived and time was passed with the customary questions about each others' school and current practice as they awaited the arrival of someone of some eminence to steer proceedings in a more productive direction.

It was about ten minutes later that the door opened and two senior members of staff entered: the first, a bushy-haired, moustached, dark suited chap complete with folders, sheets and a purposeful authoritative air. The second, a taller, younger fellow – also in collar and tie but of more casual design, indicative of a more easy-going, likely more junior rank.

The first introduced himself as a First Deputy. He spoke in quick bursts of energy that seemed entirely in-keeping with his hunch-shouldered business-like manner.

'Right I have some details here which I'd like to hand to each of you,' he said, speaking in a distinctly brusque, business-like tone. He passed the A4 pieces of paper round quickly – a little too quickly – as two slid off to the floor and disappeared under a table. He watched them disappear from sight, briefly contemplating the implications of retrieving them before opting to move on, returning his attention to the remaining sheets.

'I have several spares here,' he said, reassuring them that proceedings were not going to be interrupted by a few sheets sliding to the floor. 'This just gives you some background information on the school – catchment details – and some information on the basic pastoral structure and organisation.'

He passed them round watching and waiting till the last candidate had taken possession.

No school – or likely any organisation of comparable size and structure – would be complete without its in-house 'buffoon': one – or possibly two – usually senior and, quite often male – character(s) whose chief contribution to proceedings appears to be to throw the operation into a state of confusion at any given opportunity and, in so doing, provide an endless source of amusement for the staffroom regulars at lunchtime. Which is not to say that he, or she, need necessarily be unpopular: 'nice guy' and 'buffoon' are far from incompatible epithets on many a school's staffing list.

He was such a character. On this occasion his 'buffoonery' was failing to ensure he had the appropriate papers in hand, prompting a moment or two's confusion and whispers with his colleague, before he scuttled off to get more information, leaving the Head Of Department to fill in further details and the candidates to do their bit to convey a bit of nous by asking appropriate questions.

He returned full of smiles and brandishing the day's agenda in his hand: First, an informal chat with himself and the HOD. which was of course already underway, and could almost be ticked off now….good. This would be followed by a short walk across the building for formal interviews with the Head in his room.

He took a seat, crossed his legs, looked at his notes, and adopting as serious a countenance as he could muster, began to convey a positive image of the school's current state-of-play. He quoted encouragingly (if somewhat selectively) – from recent reports: *areas of improvement…good practice* conveniently omitting such prefixes as *need for…* and *occasional…*adding that: in recent years the school had established a 'good solid base' which they were in the process of building on and there was a 'positive atmosphere' throughout the school and a recognition of the value of learning on the part of most pupils. Following a question on the thorny issue of discipline, he quickly assured them that no pupils would be allowed to disrupt the learning of others, though he was noticeably less forthcoming as to how this was actually achieved.

It was predictably vacuous stuff, and largely a pack of lies.

It is a sign of the times that many – if not the majority – of schools will lay claim to 'not allowing pupils' behaviour to interrupt the learning of others' whilst knowing full well that it goes on day in day out – in a significant number of their classrooms and to an often quite alarming degree – and, equally commonly, without having the faintest idea as to what to do about it.

But of course, as a humble interviewee, you simply sit, bide your time and play the game.

With that part of the day's agenda firmly ticked, they set off down the corridor on the short – though, arguably, not short enough – walk to the Head's office.

Evidence of the school's 'good practice' and 'solid base' was fairly thin on the ground in a number of the classrooms they passed, where battles for vocal and territorial supremacy appeared to be the order of the day.

Two pupils, temporarily denied the benefits of learning by being removed from the classroom, were spotted standing by their respective doors, each bearing obligatory expressions of bored recalcitrance.

All of which posed something of a dilemma for The Deputy who wouldn't have wanted the interviewees to see pupils excluded from lessons, but couldn't he be seen to breeze past them without offering some sort of intervention. Unfortunately, being a buffoon, he had little awareness of his shortcomings, particularly in dealing one-to-one with recalcitrant pupils, seeing only an opportunity to: *one*...display a masterful air and *two*...impress the candidates with just how one goes about dealing with these situations.

He approached the boy first. Denying himself the benefits of learning appeared to be a minor consideration; the boy's defence being that...'it weren't his fault', 'he always gets picked on' and an insistence that the teacher was a 'prick'. All of which threw the deputy into a state of some confusion, prompting a quick resort to the tried and trusted Plan B: some vacuous closing comment followed by a hasty retreat.

With a grimace and a quick brush of his lapels, he joined the group and they continued on their way.

Unfortunately, his prowess in the pastoral arena was to be put to the test once more by a second pupil, a girl further down the corridor who had also seen fit to deny herself the benefits of learning by being removed from the class.

She stared at the floor in sulky defiance as the Deputy approached and did a quick mental count to three.

He started with the uniform.

Most will be aware of the majority of schools' – particularly secondary schools' – inclination to ape public schools by dressing their pupils in as strict a uniform as is feasible, in the hope (or expectation) that – in line with the national maxim 'older' = 'better' – their establishment will automatically acquire an aura of 'excellence'. And the more silly – stripy blazers, silly hats and any other vestiges of a bye-gone era that can be conjured up – the more 'excellent' the school will be deemed to be.

What isn't so well known is that in all these schools, there are in fact, *two* uniforms: the school dictating the garments and colour, and the pupils dictating *how* they should be worn in order to gain peer-group acceptance.

The girl in question had devoted time and energy in adapting former to latter: her skirt hovering somewhere round the lower end of her arse, her tie stubbed to a dishevelled knot hanging loosely round a slack, unbuttoned collar.

Under his directive, the tie was grudgingly returned to some semblance of order and she made an unconvincing commitment to wearing the correct skirt tomorrow [though whether he'd check up on this was doubtful because: one - he didn't make a note of it to remind him, which he ought to have done, being so absent-minded, which was further evidence that/and; two – he was a 'buffoon'.]

Again, denying herself the benefits-of-learning appeared to cut little ice. She mumbled some semi-audible dirge about 'not 'avin' done nothing", and having 'done the crappy worksheet last year', prompting a quick reminder of the expectation of certain standards and a second hasty retreat to rejoin his entourage on their way to the Head's office.

As the candidates sat waiting patiently to be summoned to the 'main act', the interviewee couldn't help but smile at the glaring contrast of the formality of the proceedings that would follow, with the atmosphere of disorder and chaos that ran through much of the building behind them; enough certainly to enable him to prepare quite detailed answers to the likely questions. He read his book and waited.

When it was his turn he followed the Deputy past two doors to an open door leading into a large, quite comfortable room flanked by shelves and sideboard and with a large wooden table placed almost centrally.

The Head was a weasely-looking man – a little on the short side with a callow face and weak expression. He shook hands, somewhat limply and, in a flaccid, slightly high-pitched voice, introduced his colleagues: the Head Of Department he'd already met; the Chairman Of The Governors - a dapper-looking guy wearing the dubious white collar on a coloured shirt – you'd see him selling second-hand cars as soon as interviewing teachers and The Borough Advisor – a non-entity of an individual who nodded briefly and proceeded to leaf through the notes he'd been issued with.

The interviewee took his seat, crossed his legs and leant back for things to start happening.

Having introduced the cast, the Head leafed through a number of sheets in front of him – evidence on candidates' behalf – and some maybe not.

He summarised the interviewee's current post and position and brushing his fingertips together and leaning back, he asked him, in a thin winsome voice that had some difficulties coping with the letter r, to describe the qualities he'd bring to the school. He then reclined, waiting to see how the chap would shape up to his first hurdle.

By way of reply, the candidate detailed certain areas of experience and expertise that he hoped would contribute to a new department, should he be offered the chance to become a part of it. It seemed a safe enough answer – spoken in a confident but not overly strident voice – and was followed by nodding agreement at the Head's assertion that we certainly cannot afford to stand still in education; we need to be constantly revising our methodology and current practice in the light of new demands and techniques – which was very well put.

They moved on. In the next question he was asked why he sought a move to this school.

He mirrored the Head's posture – sitting back with arms folded and began to speak at some length about his current school's increasing problems in areas of discipline: a key concern being the apparent unwillingness of the management team to accept there was a problem – teachers, of course, had to take responsibility as far as they were able – but support and leadership must come from the top.

He paused, checking for any reaction from the panellists – but there was little beyond a few shifting eyes and a bowed head.

He continued, citing the mounting concern in many schools regarding pupils' behaviour and the unwillingness of some headteachers to accept it – either because they're ill-equipped to do so, or simply too weak, and therefore unwilling to do so.

The Head stared down at his papers, the advisor tapped on the table and the school governor stared out of the window.

He concluded by pointing out the appalling scenario in one school – he wasn't sure which one, but a school in the area – where a teacher had been assaulted and the Head had urged everyone to keep it quiet to avoid any negative publicity and protect the school's reputation in the local community.

'Can anyone imagine any headteacher being so gutless and pathetic?'

A good question. One that prompted a self-conscious cough and a pause, as the Head thought for a moment and then, still staring down at his notes, informed the 'candidate' that the interview was over and that under the circumstances it would probably be best if he left the premises immediately.

The interviewee smiled and rose to his feet, announcing that he had every intention of leaving the premises immediately because he had no intention of working in a place like this. He added that he hoped the Head and his colleagues had gained something from the interview even though things hadn't gone entirely their way.

As he rose, he turned to face the panel.

'In some schools headmaster, the senior management have more to learn than any of their pupils. Thank you for your time.' At which point he turned to make his exit.

The Head coughed and, looking down at his list, suggested that they get the next candidate in.

[Over recent decades – and likely before – it has been the practice of some schools to attempt to conceal cases of severe ill-discipline, including, in some cases, abuse and assaults on staff, in order to avoid the adverse publicity that might follow.]

On The Way Home
From Work One Day

Jed Sparrow kicked a dried furl of wood across the baked earth and hitched his cap a little higher on his brow. He kicked again – the baggy dungarees flapping irritably around his ankles, whilst behind, his buddy Gus Heller – a slower, lumbering guy with stooping shoulders hunched forwards in an attempt to keep up the pace, swivelling his cap to release some of the heat that had been gathering around his forehead and ears. Their talk was limited: the new boss who'd taken over from Sam, the new gal working the canteen and the 'goddamn heat' that had they could swear been around longer than either of them, hovering around them like a steam-bath, forcing them to take regular wipes of foreheads necks and jowls.

'Sonofabitch.' Jed dabbed at the trickles dribbling his neck from the lower strands of hair. Gus picked up on the act, brushing an arm across his broad expanse of forehead.

They came to a fork in the lane; one way heading to the Brewer ranch, the other to a thicket of shacks and a hardware and grocery store. The pair fell into a lazy silence as they trudged past the store to lines of dusty hedgerows and flat empty cornfields – all as still as graveyards in the thick afternoon heat. They stopped only occasionally, raising a nose to the clouds that could be thickening to a storm in the north and to let a little heat escape from around their collar. And to eye the first signs of what seemed to be some commotion a hundred yards or so up the lane – far from clear at that distance, but close enough to have them step up the pace a fraction.

They passed a handful of sheds, a few chicken-runs and garage yard before venturing to a fenced-off pen to the side of the lane. The buzz was focused on the near side of the sheds. They drew in, making for a familiar standpoint at one of the posts, close to the fringe of the lane.

The scene was a familiar one. Across the pen, they could see a man (or 'boy' more likely) perched under the bough of a tree in a clearing set back to some forty or fifty feet to the left of a barn. As they moved into place, the boy shrivelled visibly, probably no more than fifteen or sixteen – a slip of a kid on closer examination. The men at his side were oblivious to the boy's age – they were more focused on getting the final preparations right.

Back on the lane, a second line of men leant passively against the fence waiting for proceedings to begin. Only occasionally would the silence be broken, blank expressions sufficient communication in light of the events to follow. Bill Jordan, one of Jed's partners at the mill threw a hand in their direction. And next to him, Joe Davis from the hardware store and Mike Elder, son of a rancher over Hallas and then Frank Butcher from the main store up toward the top of the road.

Their greetings, though amicable enough, were subdued, each aware that on afternoons such as this, everything that needed to be said was waiting there right ahead in the centre of the paddock.

The boy was standing on a stool. He was sixteen years of age and lived – or had lived – all his life just a few miles away in a tumbledown shack with his parents out beyond the river-banks – a low-lying area, firm enough in the height of summer, but prone to regular flooding once the rains started. His pose was increasingly restless: all-too-brief reflection of an all-too-brief existence: an existence that had amounted to little beyond trailing the river banks and turnip fields, occasionally hoeing the corn or helping with the potatoes out beyond the broom-sedge. Like many of their generation, it was a life borne out of solitude: days spent wandering the fields, a little fishing when the river was up or watching the swallows diving along the puffs of wind that would take them from the unplowed fields to the long brown banks of the river. And at the end of the day, if the sun had dipped, maybe take its place in its shadows and watch the girls – the pretty girls skipping their way from town or from the cotton mill at the far end of the valley. He'd remember the girls; their skirts hollering, their screams loud and raucous calling from the roadside. But at that moment he was too terrified to think of any of that. He was about to be hanged and was doing his utmost to keep all those things out of his mind.

His feet had been tied and he was flanked by two men who were busy testing a length of rope dangling behind the branch of the pecan tree just behind where he was standing.

The man, or boy, about to be hanged was a negro. He said nothing or appeared to be saying nothing – it was difficult to say from that distance. He appeared to be doing little beyond staring at the distant mountains, their jagged, snow-capped peaks a reminder of the far-off places his grandpa used to tell him about when he was a kid.

Gus eased himself into place against the fence and nodded in the direction of the tree.

'What'd he do?'

Joe eyed the figure stood motionless on the stool.

'Bin givin' them big lips little too much exercise,' he said, grinning – open invitation for others to join in the joke.

'Been listening to too many o' them 'black-snake blues' his daddy been wangin' out of his banjo on the balcony after sundown,' said Frank, a local cow-hand, shifting a few feet to get himself in on the action.

'Bout time these nigger-boys got the message,' said Mike, a younger member of the Hallas ranch, opting to dispense with the humour – his expression fixed only on the scene ahead, a stalk of grass rolling continuously from one side of his mouth to the other.

The observation was sufficient to have all eyes locked in the same direction – universal acknowledgement that a death was about to occur here; and you always found time for a moment of death – especially a nigger's – if only to see him swinging high and dry in the air like a jack-rabbit.

It was a few minutes later that at a signal from one of the men, they looked across to see the rope being lowered over the boy's head and down onto his shoulders.

Mike Elder waited for the rope to settle into place and turned to his left.

'Guess it's your turn Jed?'

Jed had had his eye fixed on the boy waiting on the stool for some time.

The invitation had him ease himself from the fence and make his way to the gate, where the men parted, allowing his unhindered passage. The few standing at the boy's side also took a few paces back. The stage was set – the rope already secured round the boy's neck.

Jed made his way to the boy's side and after fixing him a quick stare, turned his eye to the stool. He didn't look up again. Instead, he did a quick count, and in a move designed to catch everyone unawares – including the boy – he made a quick grab for the stool, yanking it from under the boy's feet to send it scuttling in the grass. He stepped back in time to watch the boy drop, his neck jolting against the rope, yanking him to a sudden standstill, where, after a moment's gagging and twitching, he was left swinging limply from the branch. A moment's silence was followed by a closer investigation.

Jed turned to a smattering of hand-claps and hoots from beyond the fence. He made his way back to Gus. He did not look back. Behind him, the men had already closed in to lift the stool and take it to one side. They would wait a little longer before taking the boy down. It was the signal for the dusting down of hats and the exodus to begin, joining the drift back up the lane.

The saloon was ready, proceedings about to begin.

Bill Jordan led the way, his hat slung over his shoulder. Joe drew himself from the rear to take his appointed place at the front of the queue, where he flopped against the counter and eased the hat from his brow. Joe waited for him to settle into place, raising a glass.

'Here's to the little nigger – who kissed the girls 'n made 'em cry?' he said, emptying the glass's contents with a single flick of the wrist.

One of the cow-hands leant forward.

'That what he done then....the kid?'

Joe nodded, his eye drawn to a passing bottle. He took it and emptied some of its contents into a glass. And then looked over the other shoulder.

'Kissing some girl in the middle of a cornfield – the pair of 'em just sittin' there, kissin' away like two racoons caught in a bear trap.'

'Had her held flat,' said Frank, extending his arms aside of the bar.

'Would 've raped her if he ain't 've been seen,' said Mike.

Voices of confirmation were thwarted only by the keys of the piano springing to life at the far side of the room. The men looked over to where two dancers were already taking their place at the end of the bar.

'Take a drink Jed.'

Jed emerged from the far side of the bar to see a Bourbon-on-the-rocks appear from nowhere and Mike encouraging him to claim ownership before it fell into foreign hands.

He took it and raised it to two figures standing at the back, peering approvingly through a sea of faces, his own eye skirting the scene of half-empty glasses and half-raised conversations. Gus emerged from behind, two more glasses pressed into a fist. He laid one in Jed's direction and leant closer to his friend's ear.

'Did I tell ya 'bout a preacher.....Preacher Dave they call him. You know the guy?'

He moved closer in an attempt to veil his voice from the hustle and bustle behind.

Jed took a mouthful of beer and nodded – largely a gesture of appeasement midst the growing hubbub around them.

Gus's voice rose as if to keep time with the rhythm of piano keys behind.

'Well anyway, I see the guy– the preacher – standing in the truck, you know – actually *standing* in the truck. I figure maybe he's layin' on a sermon – or baptising a kid, somethin' like that. But....know what the guy was doin'?

The question remained purely rhetorical – hoots and hollers from the dance-floor would see to that. 'He's sellin' shirts. No word of a lie. Stuck on the highway; standin' there shakin' a bunch of shirts like he's preachin' 'gainst hell and damnation, like some dealer from Clarkesville.'

The laughter rose and quickly faded, aided by the piano keys springing back to life at the far side of the bar.

Jed took another drink and stood a moment eyeing the huddled figures and muffled conversations, and then turned to the doorway, where the light was already signalling the rapid approach of night. By his reckoning it would be half an hour's walk back home, being something of an hour's detour to get here in the first place. He glanced at his watch and nudged Gus, placing the empty glass on the table.

'Gonna be making a move.' He slapped his buddy on the shoulder. Gus nodded but showed little indication of following him. Instead, he raised another beer, levelling it at his friend.

'One for the road,' he said finally. The men exchanged looks and Jed took the glass and raised it to meet Gus's. Seconds later, it was returned to the nearest table. Jed took his hat from the chair and signalled a few greetings to those near enough to acknowledge them.

Once outside, he stood a moment taking advantage of a little space. Though the night was warm, the air was cool and welcoming after the stifling heat of the bar. The scene down the lane had mostly shrunk from sight, the fence little more than a shadow in the corner of the field, the tree just another vague shape beneath the rapidly emerging stars. There was no sign of the boy.

He turned and settled into a steady stride, passing the grocery store and rows of shuttered windows, their lights burning like lines of tiny fires. The events of the day suddenly behind him, he found himself quickening his pace. He guessed it would take him forty or fifty minutes along the cotton-mill road to home.

As he approached the house he looked across the cluster of apple trees and the stretch of sweet potatoes, seeing if he could catch his wife busying herself in or around the room. She was nowhere to be seen. Only a small light was partly visible, leaking from the table in the hallway.

He made his way along the path and opened the door to the kitchen. A small dog rustled its way across the floor to brush against his feet. He leant a moment to brush a hand against its back and made his way into the room.

First impression was the whole place was deserted. He made for the counter to stick the water on the hob and take a hunk of bread from the bin at its side. The light from the hallway seeped its way to the door to settle on the window, beyond which, lay the depths of the thicket and the potato plants.

A shadow spread into the light, and seconds later, his wife appeared framed in the hallway.

He looked up to catch her eye and for a moment no words passed between them. She had a towel slung over her forearm and her hair was tied into a bun, out of the way of the evening's chores. He waited for some sign of recognition. He guessed straight off that she was feeling a little sore. She sniffled and made for the sink, draping the towel across a nearby chair-back.

'Bit late huh?' She leant into the sink and reached for a plate. He had taken his seat and backed himself lazily against the wall.

'Stopped for a couple o' beers with the guys.' He flicked a newspaper in front of his face. His wife turned from the sink and reached for a nearside cupboard. She was looking into the window, picking out his reflection in the oval of orange light.

He looked up, sensing the direction her questioning might be heading.

'Didn't stay long, okay; just a couple o' beers and a few shots.' He flicked the page of his paper in a gesture of minor irritation. 'Susie home?' He knew they needed to change the subject but felt no inclination to look up from the paper. His wife failed to reply for a moment and took a pot from the stove to the counter.

Susie was their daughter, an only child. Sixteen years of age and still growing, or so it seemed. Fetching looks, inherited by popular consensus from her mother. A brooding, lonesome child, never more evident than at the nearby cotton-mill where he she had recently been obliged to take up work: a bustling, hostile place, full of wailing machines and strange, hostile people, the only sound to raise her spirits – the end-of-shift bell: the moment when she could finally make her escape across the fields to the rabbits and the birds soaring and diving along the puffs of wind on their way down to the riverbanks.

His wife had remained standing by the sink, passing a towel over a bunch of plates clasped firmly in her hand. Moments later, a figure emerged in the light from the hallway.

She looked nervous, hanging on to the jamb of the door, a foot crooked under a folded leg. Her mother switched plates and kept her eye on her chores. Neither of them spoke, nor seemed inclined to break the silence.

Jed looked up. For a moment, he too was quiet and then he threw a hand invitingly in the direction of the girl.

'Hi honey.'

Her silence drew his attention back to the newspaper.

Across the room her mother gave the plate an extra wipe with the towel before she turned to look over her shoulder.

'Well, you gonna tell your daddy...'

The suggestion brought another scuffing of her foot against the floor. She retreated further into the doorway. Across the room another plate found its way to the bottom of the pile.

'It's okay....you can tell him. Tell him like you told me. He'll understand.' She quickly looked away, the towel now folded under the pile of plates.

Again there was little response. Only eventually did the words come – stumbling and tumbling, almost before she'd had time to think about it.

'We was on'y playin' – me and Joey....I din't mean nothin.' I on'y give him a little kiss. Then I see Joey jump back 'n push me away. But I din't see no folks over by the lane. First they was laughing and jokin'. Then calling stuff – sayin' stuff 'bout him gonna be a dead boy___'

She looked across, willing her father to see the point: that they were just kids, doing what kids do.

'It was o'ny a little kiss.'

She sniffed and shuffled a toe against the broken tile.

'Will you tell 'em daddy? Tell 'em I din't mean nothin'. That they should leave me 'n Joey alone. That all I done was give him a little kiss___?'

She stopped, assured that he would understand. This was – after all – what fathers were for.

Her mother had fallen silent. She knew that the last thing her daughter would dream of doing was anything to cross him. The plates temporarily forgotten, she watched her husband's eye drift to the cluster of apple trees stretching into the darkness beyond the window.

'Don't worry honey.....I'll tell 'em.....' he said.

Margarita

Thomas Harbinger took a familiar stance in front of his window and stared across the night-time panorama of the city. He drew deeply on a cigarette, flopped an occasional ash into a lid, and turned his eye back into the room, and to Margarita behind him on the sofa, reclining into the folds of the cushion.

It was to be their first evening together; an evening that had begun some time ago with a ten minute schlep to the tube station followed by a short train journey, and then the interminable clamber up the stairs, puffing and panting their way to the top, where they'd paused to catch their breath and take stock of their first real moments 'together' whilst he'd searched for the clump of keys in his pocket.

Once inside and with the preliminaries sorted, first on the agenda had been a cup of tea. You can't get round to anything when you get home of a night before the all-important cup of tea. Margarita concurred and he wasted no time in getting the kettle steaming, and the two cups at the ready.

It felt strange to be standing alone in the alcove of his kitchenette, waiting for the kettle to boil, knowing a woman was waiting for him, not twenty feet away; waiting and no doubt trying to get her bearings – familiarising herself with her new surroundings

With the teabags drained and dumped in the swing-bin, he returned to the room and leant over the chair arm to place her cup on the rickety table next to the sofa, bringing them eyeball to eyeball – their heads almost touching – and for a while that's how they remained, mutual acknowledgement of each other's presence, until, drawing himself back to full height, he made for his seat across the room – her eyes following his every step.

Later he would join her on the sofa, but not yet, there was plenty of time and he didn't want to give the impression of trying to rush things. He needed to give her time to get settled and drink her tea – content himself with the occasional glance in her direction. He guessed she wouldn't mind; more likely take some pride in the fact that he liked looking at her.

But he also knew it was down to him to keep things moving, to avoid them drifting into one of those awkward silences that can kill an evening stone dead.

He took the opportunity to tell her about himself – about the flat – being there seventeen years, never having moved because of all the hassle, there never seeming to be much point. About the flat upstairs; washing machines dripping through the ceiling, Romanian gypsies – who never slept and spent their nights rowing and smashing the place up, until one day they disappeared and didn't come back.

Even as he was speaking, he could sense her looking round, taking it all in: the cracks in the walls, the bare patch in the middle of the carpet; the makeshift cupboard, nailed together and rapidly coming apart at the seams, the line of bottles, left to gather dust at the far end of the sink. The place was a bit grubby, he'd have to admit that, and a bit chilly in winter but it had its own kitchen area and a sink and the sofa that she was sitting on. And the bed was okay although it tended to sag a bit in the middle. He wouldn't tell her about that; they'd maybe come to that later.

He rose with the offer of another cup of tea and a quick decision to get into the bathroom now, while it was free; to get that bit over and done with, though he'd still likely need some persuading. He hated it: standing there bare-topped under a few hundred kilowatts of light; flesh hanging over his belt like folds of pastry – pale stilted thighs. Goodness knows what Margarita would think.

For some reason it seemed to take even longer than usual, until, with a final check that that the bristle had been fully erased, he made his way back to the kitchen and to the room where Margarita had barely moved, sitting there framed in the shadows from the lamp and the tv set.

He resumed his seat, trying to make a point of seeming casual and relaxed, slouching in his seat, taking only fleeting glimpses at the tv screen, yet mindful of the need to keep things moving so she wouldn't start feeling neglected and maybe think about leaving.

He told her about his family; about his mother and father who lived in Shrewsbury, who he hadn't seen for two and a half years; how he'd never really got on with them, being a bit of a disappointment to them, not having married and having no family or proper job or nice house to live in with its own garden. He told her about their house, a big house on the bend in a quiet avenue. How his father was quite rich and short-tempered, and had a thing about people 'wasting their opportunities' and 'failing to make the most of their lives'. About his mother being incredibly fussy, and appalled when she'd once come to visit him in his last flat – a bedsit-room with two cooking rings and mice that used to visit in the middle of the night and take chunks from his loaf of bread. It had been her one and only visit and one visit too many as far as she was concerned. She hadn't liked the area either and commented on how many 'non-whites' there were. She called them 'non-whites' because she thought it was the best way to put it, rather than Pakistanis or Blacks. His father said 'Coloureds' was another way of putting it – but whatever way you put it, they didn't approve, so it didn't really make much difference.

He suddenly realised he'd been talking a lot and felt a bit guilty about going on about his family like that, maybe boring her or turning her off because of him talking about the 'non-whites', not that Margarita was a 'non-white', she was definitely 'white', you could tell that a mile off. Anyway, she hadn't said anything and didn't seem to mind.

He asked if she wanted another cup of tea, because he was going to get one and it would be impolite not to ask if she wanted one too. He went back into the kitchen to put the kettle on. Time was getting on. Soon be time to make his move and go and sit down beside her.

He spooned the sugar and reached for the milk, listening for any signs of disturbance behind. Margarita was certainly a quiet one, there was no doubt about that. But he didn't mind that, he liked quiet women and she certainly liked her tea. He gave the bags a few extra squeezes, taking a second to watch the brown dye ooze to the correct shade in the cups.

On his return, he made a point of standing behind her, watching the light catching the curves in her cheeks and the tiny dots peppered in clusters at their centre. That's what had struck him when he'd first set eyes on her – the tiny freckles on her cheeks.

He strode nonchalantly across the room, where he made a point of stopping and with half an eye on Margarita, stooped to drape the lamp with a tee-shirt. He wanted it to be right: low-key like in a film.

With the light dimmed he made his way back across the room to flop down beside her, reaching across to make his move.

He drew her to him, relishing the warmth and closeness of touch, her cheek resting neatly in the brace of his neck; a finger tracing tiny figures of eight across her bare arm. Moments later, he rose again, this time to cross the room and extinguish the lamp once and for all.

Stumbling in the semi-darkness, he resumed his seat and lifting her hand from her knee, squeezed it gently, his other hand rising to the porcelain-smoothness of her cheek, tilting it towards him to close his lips over the soft oval of her mouth.

With each kiss came the systematic release of the cheesecloth's buttons, her eyes rapidly transforming into wild, staring digits – her fingers splayed and idle, allowing him to fumble the flaps apart. She wasn't wearing a bra. Adjusting his posture he could just about make out the twin cairns – perfectly spaced like freshly plopped blancmanges, their tips bright and glistening like glace cherries. He closed his lips over first one, and then the other – teasing each against his tongue which he later retracted to facilitate an avid sucking motion, mindful of the need not to bite too hard. He completed the undressing, sliding the top from her shoulders. Within seconds her skirt was down, and off.

He entered her surprisingly easily – up to the hilt in little more than a few quick stabs, her voice stabbing back at him – urging him to find that rapid three/four time against the back of the sofa, and to hold it there until the time was right, until the steady pistoning rhythm had time to make its mark. He gave it his best shot but, as is often the case, he couldn't quite make it – and with a grimace and a swift arching of his back, he brought proceedings to a halt fractionally before the bell.

It took a moment to resume their former positions, nestled into each others' shoulders, her arm draped effortlessly across his. It had been a taxing business and a return-trip, though a possibility, would certainly have to wait a while. At that moment what he needed more than anything was a cigarette.

It took a further gargantuan effort to reach down, grab the packet and raise one of its contents to his lips, flicking the lighter to bring the cigarette to life and Margarita's cavernous features back into the frame.

Nestled in the crook of her shoulder he inhaled deeply – one hand raised to the soft curvature of her cheek – the other shielding the cigarette in the narrow slot that lay between them.

It was as he made a move to meet the soft portal of her lips that the cigarette – left to its own devices a little too long – moved in too, first brushing against – then stabbing into – the upper reaches of her left thigh.

Within seconds he was out of his seat – up and in the centre of the room. But it was too late: he was left with little option than to stand and watch in blank astonishment, as – midst a series of gasps and two thin pencil-lines of smoke – Margarita keeled to one side, crumpled and finally withered to a streak of plastic draped over the arm of the chair.

At first glance it was difficult to take it all in: that a fully fledged, full-blown woman could – in the space of a few seconds – become little more than a shrivelled mat flopped across the arm of the sofa.

He moved closer, turning an accusing eye on the still-smouldering stem of the cigarette, making his way round the back of the chair, following the furrows and folds in the flattened curvature of her body: the wrinkled pods of her breasts, the face – still chirpy and open-mouthed – but now hung back and staring obscenely at the ceiling.

Then he made his way to the window, eventually managing to open it to allow the heady mix of smoke and molten plastic to disappear above the city skyline.

And for some moments that's where he remained, following the weaving patterns ebb and flow against the clusters of lights – before turning back to the room, and to Margarita, flopped across the arm, as flat and useless as an old inner-tube.

It seemed such a waste. And he'd had it all worked out: tomorrow – a cup of coffee down the road and maybe a stroll in the park. Back for tea and an early-evening sex session.

Then the following weekend; he'd got that worked out too: a surprise appearance at the country pub near Shrewsbury where his parents went every Sunday for lunch after church – a big pub with a garden and play-area for kids.

He'd have liked to have seen their faces – the expressions of amazement when he turned up, out of the blue, with a woman, after all these years. It would have been a sight to behold. But, alas, it would have to wait.

He looked beyond Margarita, trying to recall whether there was a beer in the fridge. He could do with a beer after everything that had happened.

In the morning he'd have to carry her back down the stairs to put her in the bin on his way back into town. But that was tomorrow. He stubbed the cigarette out in the lid and made his way to the kitchenette, to check the beer situation, and put the kettle on.

Coming Again

It was as the final carriage of the 14:52 'Midland-Express' service slipped past the tail-end of the platform, that Harold Warburton sensed all wasn't as it should be – a driver's sixth sense being quick to pick up on the slightest interruption to his routine – be it a fly bobbing and weaving around the cab or some unexpected movement over his right shoulder.

On this occasion, it was quite definitely the latter: a young to middle-aged man, maybe late twenties, early thirties, standing almost to attention over his right shoulder sharing the view out of the cabin's front window.

To Harold Warburton, this was a first. Leaves on the ground, snow emergencies, even – sad though it was to have to contemplate it – a 'jumper' leaping into space ahead of him, were scenarios that, with varying degrees of likelihood, he might be expected to encounter. But someone standing over your shoulder in the cabin?.....The cabin was locked for Christ's sake – they all were these days – or supposed to be!

Initial impression was a man of slimmish build though it was difficult to be sure, given that most of him was drowned in an ankle length great coat – Asian, or Asianish – certainly not entirely white. He wore a thin waspish beard and unkempt hair reaching to just above his shoulders. Eyes were blue or blueish, with, he had already observed, a kind of empty, glazed look.

Initial reaction – as much a defensive gesture as anything, might have been to spread himself across the throttle and gauges. But for some reason, he didn't. Instead, he simply turned to his right, and in as flat and detached a voice as he could muster, asked the man what he thought he was up to, and to explain his appearance through a door that, in states of transit, was permanently locked.

The man listened, and out of deference, turned an eye on the offending door. Then turned again, this time to speak.

'I simply made my way through the train, and then opened the door and walked through it.'

'The door's locked,' said the driver immediately and emphatically.

The man looked again at the article in question but simply shrugged. It was there, and he'd opened it; it was as simple as that.

'You know you're trespassing,' the driver added, one eye checking for sudden hints of movement, the other following the curve in the line ahead. 'Entry to this cab is strictly forbidden to members of the public and....to anyone other than officially licensed personnel or employees of the company...' He was almost surprising himself at his ability to quote so directly from the manual.

To the man it seemed less of an issue; certainly not enough to draw his eye from the passing buildings or from delving a hand into his right coat pocket – a move that brought the driver quickly back to his senses.

'What you got there?' he asked, an eye poised on a hand about to appear clutching God knows what.

The man withdrew his hand, revealing what appeared to be a ball of clingfilm.

'Luncheon,' he explained, raising the small cellophane package to view.

The driver was far from placated; there was some funny business going on here, and someone, somewhere, needed to get to the bottom of it.

'You're going to face arrest,' he said, his voice hovering somewhere on the brink between a threat and a warning. 'You realise that, don't you?'

The man said nothing. The unwrapping was nearing completion, and he was pre-occupied enough in trying to establish the true nature of what he was about to consume.

It was only after a few private words and a brief hiatus to digest the opening bites, that he turned again to the driver, conceding that perhaps a little explanation might be in order.
'The thing is....' he said, screwing the clingfilm into a tiny ball and slotting it into his pocket......
'I'm Jesus.'

He tapped the pocket and turned his eye once more to the cab's front window.

The explanation, simple and direct though it was, cut little ice with the driver. Nor did it explain his sudden and inappropriate appearance in the cab.
'What do you mean Jesus? Jesus who?'
The man looked across with the look of a patient uncle.
'*The* Jesus.'

The driver's eye had been busily flitting between the line and diminishing conglomerations of housing blocks – a sure sign that their departure from the City was imminent. Though unquestionably a patient man, it was a patience that had come to know its limits, and certainly fell short of passing the time of day with lunatics – Biblical or otherwise – who wandered at will through locked doors into the cabin of his train.
'Jesus Christ,' the man confirmed, brushing his hands and casting his own eye on the rapidly disappearing tower-blocks through the cab's front window.

The driver shook his head.
'You're talking bollocks,' he said, quick to establish the fact that that this was *his* cab and that *he* was set to remain in charge of whatever occurred within it.

The man remained unmoved, content enough to munch his way through the remainder of his tuna and pickle roll, his attention devoted to avoiding flecks of fish dropping onto the cabin's floor.
'And I still don't understand how you got in here,' the driver added, his attention switching from the line to the man's vaguely non compos-mentis expression.

The man shrugged – airs of scepticism were not his concern. He'd explained the situation; it was now simply a question of waiting. He swallowed the last of his roll and took an apple from his pocket.

Harold Warburton, to his credit, was doing things pretty much by the book. Unprecedented as the scenario was, the likelihood of imminent threat appeared to be minimal. And he had met little protest in activating the 'two-way' hands-free intercom communication, in this case, with the local wing of the TRS – Terrorist Response Squad, whose members – one imagined – would be galvanised into action the minute he terminated the message. But he was still taking no chances.

A series of bleeps caught both their attention. The driver hesitated before speaking.

'Yes. I dunno. About ten minutes ago...I know it's locked, I told him that.'

A moment's delay presumed the recording of a message – a flurry of activity behind the scenes in the control system at HQ, and likely beyond....

'What? He says he's Jesus – Jesus...J-e-s-u-s. I dunno....Christ I suppose...I dunno. What? No he din't say nothing about no H...Yes, okay...'

He'd kept his eye on the man, still searching for any hint of untoward movement before the line, at least temporarily, went dead. Little remained than to see how things transpired in due passage of time.

Which – as they weaved an all-too-familiar route from the confines of the city – was something they appeared to have plenty of, prompting the driver to turn again to his fellow-traveller.

'I still don't see how you got through that door,' he said, opting, in these more convivial climes, for a slightly less confrontational approach. 'That door is locked – permanently during transit...'

The man turned again to the source of the man's disquiet.
'I had a little help,' he said, looking to the cabin's roof and nibbling a corner of apple.
'What do you mean, help?'
An eye remained skywards a moment before returning to the panel and some soon-to-be-discovered spot on the horizon. 'From my Heavenly Father,' he said, returning to the narrow space that divided them. It was the driver's turn to remain silent – for the moment.

Their destination was some fifteen miles away and a series of semi-audible beeps was the only indication of the TRS attempting to make contact with HQ or the local Transport Police. The driver, able to decipher little beyond a few inaudible grunts, abandoned the effort, mindful of the need to buy a little more time.
'You realise you're talking bollocks,' he said, an eye still fixed on saving everyone – particularly himself – a bucket-load of time, and trouble.
'And you realise you're going to face arrest.'
Jesus remained unperturbed; such matters were beyond his remit. He extended an arm to a handful of sheep idling against the perimeter wire.
'A beautiful scene,' he said, gesturing first with one arm, then the other. 'The meadows – the beasts of the fields – the trees.'
The driver's eye remained fixed on the dials and gauges before him. He was a town man, born and bred.
'So, your surname; your second name...*is* Christ then,' he said, refusing to be drawn from the issue in hand.
The man hesitated.
'It isn't as simple as that,' he said.
'What isn't?'
'The 'Christ' bit. It came later......'
'What did?'
'Christ. The name......Jesus *Christ*.'

The driver shrugged. Not being a religious man he felt little inclination to dispute the point. As far as he was concerned the man's name – Christ or otherwise, was his business. Though exactly what his business might turn out to be – having forced his way unprovoked and uninvited into the cab, and through a locked door – remained far from clear.

'So – if you're Jesus. What you doin' here?' he asked.

It was a fair question, deserving a moment's deliberation.

'Continuing the work of my Father: to teach – to lift my people from the shackles of ignorance pending sanctity in the wake of imminent apocalypse.'

The driver took a quick check on the gauges.

'You speak good English, I'll give you that. I remember that from school. Someone teach you?'

Jesus appeared not to hear, or chose not to rise to the bait. He had his eye on a second ring of sheep gathered for a moment of dusk over a wire fence, and another platform zipping in and out of vision through the blur of the right-hand window.

'It's amazing – on one hand, the pace of life, and on the other – the pace of movement,' he said, passing an eye over the next wave of hills and thickets of trees, returning only eventually to the issue in question.

'My Father facilitated the gift of the major of European tongues as an aid to me resuming my work – here – in the earlier part of the twenty-first century.'

The driver eased a finger against the throttle and looked out towards the last throes of the estuary some fifteen miles to the east.

'Useful thing languages,' he said. He turned again to his right. 'I suppose you do look a bit like Jesus – but he was a bit older than you. And his hair was a bit more wavy....and washed!'

The man smiled and, in now customary fashion, prefaced his response with a perusal of the passing terrain.

'Beauty seeks only the discerning mind,' he said. 'I *am* Jesus.'

He was clearly determined to stick to his story. But the driver was equally determined.

'So, this work you say you're doing. What work is it exactly?'

The question was again awarded a moment's contemplation, and prompted the appearance of two biscuits from his coat pocket, one of which he broke in half. He raised his left hand. 'Would you care to share in the embodiment of the flesh?'

The driver eyed the broken offering and returned to the arrows and statistics displayed on the panel before him.

'No thanks...I'm not a biscuit man.'

A corner was popped off and steady chewing commenced. It would take time to be fully digested. A second portion was raised to the window and cocked in the direction of the driver's eye.

'In answer to your question, I shall meet people – in the streets, the market-places, the back yards and town squares; wherever my people are to be found.'

He bit into the kernel, taking care to avoid spilling crumbs and then turned, and with a solid flick of his arm, propelled the apple core through the open window, its narrow-arced parabola disappearing somewhere amongst the bales of grass. The driver remained silent for a minute. He had one eye on the dial and the other on his watch.

'I'll tell you where you're going wrong,' he said finally. 'Your colour...I'm not being funny or racialist, but you're the wrong colour.'

The man made a quick perusal of his extended arms.

'Colour?'

'Colour....to be Jesus,' said the driver. 'Skin colour. I'm not being funny but you seem to be Pakistani or Indian, or from somewhere round those parts. You're too dark. You should have checked that out – with the books.'

The stare persisted.

The driver, sensing the upper hand, pressed on.

'Do you see my point?'

A moment's confusion quickly passed.

'Maybe,' came the reply.

For a while the silence held: opportunity for a little reflection and to take stock of a re-emerging landscape of rooftops and back-to-back gardens – the next bastion of civilisation already within their sights.

Having completed his lunch, the man set his hand contemplatively on the panel and turned to the driver.

'So – you say I'll be facing arrest,' he said.

'Quite likely,' said the driver, his eye focused on an array of approaching signals.

'.....for seeking to offer my people sanctity in the wake of pending apocalypse?'

The driver looked across the cab.

'For busting through the cab door,' he said. 'You're breaking all the regulations – no members of the public are permitted in this part of the train.'

Eyes turned once more to the offending article, now firmly closed behind them.

'I told you – I had a little help,' the man said.

The driver shrugged.

'Cos you're Jesus.'

The man nodded and extended a finger along the length of the panel. He had been observing the change of scenery: a stark reminder that for all the picture-book tranquillity behind them, ahead was where the 'people' and all their futures lay; a future likely laden with any number of unforeseen hurdles. He turned again to the driver.

'So – you know something about me – so much is clear.'

The driver's eye shifted suspiciously.

'What do you mean?'

'What I say.'

'I ain't a religious man,' put in the driver, quick to set the record straight.

'Tis of little consequence. The path laid down by My Father isn't by rights the easiest of paths. You're clearly versed to some degree in my life and times.'

'Well.........You say you're Jesus____'

'I *am* Jesus,' he pointed out.

'Okay....You say you're Jesus – and I still say it's bollocks – Well.....everyone knows about Jesus.'

The man stared hard at the approaching skyline, fingers planted firmly on the panel beneath him.

'Like what?' He turned to his left, his manner calm and collected. 'Tell me. I'd like to know. A lapse of two thousand years is apt to dull the memory, as I'm sure you'll appreciate.'

He was already at hand with his next question.

'Is it right for instance, that I was born in Judea? I've been given to understand as much'

The driver shrugged.

'Dunno about that,' he said. 'But *if* you was Jesus, which you ain't, you was born in Bethlehem – in a stable – in a manger – a trough where donkeys eat from.'

The smile broadened.

'And.....?'

'And what?'

'What else? I'd like to know.'

The driver shrugged, again reluctant to be put under pressure regarding such issues.

'Christmas Eve it was. Your mother was a virgin – got impregnated from above.' He looked to see the man grinning delightedly, hands hovering along the length of the panel.

'Excellent! And yet you claim *not* to be a religious man – you're clearly too modest.'

Waiting to detect any further reaction he looked ahead to where the station's angular supports and sloping roof were already visible amidst the surrounding gloom – indication, no doubt, of the trials and tribulations set to cross his path. He turned again to his left.

'So, why not come and join us? Come play a part in rescuing our people in the wake of pending apocalypse?'

The driver, already in the throes of negotiating the final approach to the station, looked up.

'I've told you – it's bollocks,' he said.

The man turned to face him.

'So – come and work with us; help lift our people from the shackles of ignorance.'

It was the driver's turn to look up.

'So...you admit it's bollocks then?'

The man smiled – not quite able to ring the words in quite so colourful a fashion, but still seeing fit to concede the point.

'Almost entirely,' he said.

The driver was smiling too. The platform was already visible some thirty yards ahead. Having slowed the train to a near crawl, he turned, prepared, in light of developments, to offer some crumb of consolation.

'What you need to remember is....When it comes to religion, you can fool some people some of the time. But you can't fool all of 'em all the time.'

The man was still smiling.

'Quite so,' he said. 'Quite so.'

At which, all eyes turned to where lines of officers were already stationed – armed and ready – along the entire length of the platform.

The driver leant across one last time.

'But – I still don't see how you got through that door,' he said.

There was a pause as Jesus reached to his pocket and produced a small metal key which he tossed nonchalantly in the driver's direction.

'Courtesy of my Heavenly Father....' he said.

Seconds later – the outer door was thrust open, and the man disappeared from view.

Down By The Riverside

Oggie and Digga stood, hands in pockets, at the foot of the towpath, Digga amusing himself with the cartoon reflections peering up at him from the pools of water, Oggie eyeing the path that would take them to the railway bridge and an abandoned barge, beyond which lay lines of barren warehouses and prison-like stretches of wall.

'Come on,' he said again, his tone one of growing impatience.

Digga had been only half-heartedly paying heed. He had been observing the fence and picturing the scene beyond it, privately speculating as to whether their time might be more gainfully spent *there* rather than alongside some crappy-looking canal.

Having reached the bridge, the pair stopped for a moment to catch the echo from its blackened roof and rain a few stones at the flotilla of cans bibbing and bobbing around the undergrowth opposite and for Oggie to reach for his cigarettes and level the packet in Digga's direction.

'Reckon a fair bit goes on under here. What do you reckon?' he said, eyeing the dubious slithers of polythene and packaging generally littering the whole area, whilst taking time out to light the cigarette from an extended hand.

'Yeh – more 'n likely,' said Digga, following his gaze and guessing as to what his friend was alluding.

Twirling the cigarette, baton-style, between his fingers – Oggie turned his attention to where the cavernous entrance of the tunnel beckoned. He looked back.

'I once fucked a bird outside. You know Kenny Barclay's sister?' Digga furrowed his brow, vague recollections stirring.

'Yeh – Kim....or Karen...something with a K.'

'Dunno, can't remember her name. Anyway, she had a mate – decent looking bird; she was in the pub – 'bout eight months ago it was – with Ken and his sister and her friend, so we got chattin'. And at the end I got 'er number and next day I rang her...met her over Cheshunt park. Went up over the Sandhills – found a little spot.' He grinned and looked across, waiting to see some reaction.

Digga had resumed his bombardment of a flotilla of cans across the water with repeatedly scant success.

'D'you give 'er one?'

Oggie nodded and watched another pebble plop its way harmlessly in the mud-banking opposite.

'We was over the other side of the quarry. It was her idea. Cos we din't 'ave nowhere else to go. But I di'nt mind.'

He stopped to level the cigarette in Digga's direction. 'As long as it was quiet. I told 'er that. But once you get past the Sandhills, across a few fields there ain't no-one around anyway, 'cept a few sheep.'

'Or some dirty bastard peering through the bushes,' Digga piped up, grinning and levelling 'o' shaped fingers and thumb in and out of his groin area.

Oggie drew a face and spat disgustedly.

'Leave it out Dig. Can you imagine?'

The pair grinned and promptly dismissed the thought.

'Ain't it 'gainst the law, fuckin' in a field? I thought you could get done for that.'

'Nah,' said Oggie, less sure of the facts than his interpretation of them. 'Long as it's a quiet field. Mind you____'

He stopped for a moment of reflection, his expression, for once, serious.

'You gotta know how to deal with them – girls....outside I mean. Some of 'em can get a bit stupid.'

He turned to the slithers of scum and polythene slapping lightly into the low wall of the canal.

'It's to do with hormones,' he said.

Digga, scrambling some distance behind, had abandoned his attempt to sink what was clearly determined to remain unsinkable.

'What, birds?' he said.

Oggie nodded and pushed on along the tunnel path, urging Digga to get a grip and stop dawdling – the girls were some way ahead and there could be difficulties were they to wander too far out of sight.

The pair edged on, occasionally venturing up the banks of grass that would eventually give way to the line of warehouse fronts – blank and forbidding against the pinks and blues of the evening sky. Neither paid much heed to the surroundings, much less what was happening above them; little in fact beyond a few cartoon reflections in the water and the next stretch of a cinder path they were guessing would bring them back out onto the open road at some point.

Oggie looked at his watch. And then ahead to a point where the canal finally broke free to ease its way alongside a series of grassy knolls and a wire fence running part of the length of the towpath, and to two figures bounding and pushing their way up and down the grassy slope before coming to a stop on the path – Hayley and Tina.

He shaded his eyes for a moment, allowing Digga time to draw level. They moved on – Oggie urging Digga to stay close.

The girls – tiring of the grassy slope, had taken respite against the railings; opportunity to catch their breath and gaze wistfully into the water and its kaleidoscope of patterns bobbing and weaving from the bank opposite.

It was only on a casual look to their left that they spotted the two ambling towards them. They exchanged glances and immediately re-directed their attention to the water. It was too late to exchange words.

Having got themselves to within hailing distance, the boys stopped, brushed themselves down and ran hands through quaffs of hair. The girls finally looked up.

'What kept ya?' said Hayley, looking at her friend and seeking to keep as healthy a distance as circumstances would permit. Oggie, brushing himself down one last time and hauling his friend alongside, offered a welcoming grin.

'Him,' he said.

The girls returned their attentions to the water.

Like the boys they were late teens, with an interesting clash in hairstyles: one close-cut, Pixie-like, the other shoulder-length peaked to a neat fringe. Oggie had made his decision when they'd first spotted them in the pub – the long-haired one would be his, the other, her friend, would be left to Digga's illustrious attentions.

The girls had been thinking too. Probably best at this early stage not to give too much away; wherever possible seek to deflect their attention elsewhere.

"orrible in it,' said Oggie, sharing their observation of the debris filtering its way in and around the canal's perimeter.

The girls nodded and exchanged glances.

Oggie flashed Digga the signal to prepare for a little tactical manoeuvring.

Leading by example, he took a few paces forward, easing himself into place, as close to Hayley as circumstances would permit, whilst following her example of resting his arms across the iron railing and, in so doing, noting – unless he was mistaken – the trace of a smile. He gave it a second or two and then leant closer.

'Fancy walkin' a bit further then?' he said.

She was looking back over her shoulder, making a point of looking round him in search of her friend. Digga – similarly disposed – was looking across too, seeking out some indication as to their next move. Hayley looked back, prepared under the circumstances, to give the proposal some consideration.

With the defensive shield gone, Oggie was quick to lay down a marker – a little voice telling him that he/they might well have finally cracked it. He sought out his friend who was busily leaning over the railing pulling faces at the reflections beaming up at him from below.

Hayley looked across and nodded.

'Okay,' she said.

Both were quickly back to their former positions – Oggie interrupting the pair to catch Digga's eye and draw him to one side, prompting Hayley to follow suit: making a quick grab for her friend's arm, dragging her several yards along the towpath. A few furtive whispers followed, after which, the pair turned in unison – their voices tinged with impatience.

'Come on then.'

Oggie, quick to assume his role as chaperone to Hayley, was first off the mark, leaving his friend to – hopefully – draw up the rear.

Within the first twenty yards things were shaping up: arms slunk through elbows, and twenty yards beyond that, the first – if, In Digga's case, somewhat tentative – holding of hands. Oggie already had an eye on his first kiss, but there was plenty of time, and he knew girls; he knew you had to pick your moment – getting it wrong could spell disaster.

They came to the first of two locks, both as dead as the warehouse that confronted them. Which was unfortunate. Water bobbing up and down with a boat on top and a few blokes tugging on ropes or whatever it was they did would have made an ideal spectacle – the first kiss a nailed-on certainty.

But it would have to wait. A few slaps of water round two slimy gates were all they were getting. That, and the opportunity to impress the girls with the clank of a few stones smacking into the rusted machinery, and a decision to move on without further ado, and for Oggie to draw an arm round Hayley's shoulder, easing her away from the danger area.

The path followed the line of the canal to a point that signalled the end of derelict buildings and the beginning of a series of grassy knolls already partly visible on the right of the pathway.

Oggie continued to lead the way, half an eye on making a quick impression, which he knew depended on there being some viable destination beyond the line of buildings – hopefully, amongst the grassy knolls, some way from the canal and – more importantly – from the nearest road.

It was about fifty yards further on that the pair hung a right, taking them to the first of a line of tiny hillocks, at which point, they looked back in time to catch Digga disappearing off to his left – Tracy in tow. Beyond them there was nothing.

For a moment the pair stood looking ahead to the next line of knolls – steeper than the others and effectively facing them away from the canal. Taking Hayley's hand he led her several feet along the path, cradling her into his shoulder to a spot safely concealed midst a bank of knee-length grass.

At which point he eased her down, settling himself on his haunches and nodding back towards the towpath.

'Fancy a swim?' He'd been saving the line for the right moment. Hayley pulled a face and looked anxiously to her right.

Oggie followed her eye. And then looked back; it was a good spot.

She was leaning forward, her arms drawn protectively around hunched up knees. Oggie, watching closely, allowed her a few moments respite.

'It's alright,' he said. 'Digga's alright – you don't need worry about them.'

She stopped to look across at the neighbouring hillocks, pulling her arms more tightly. The realisation that they were alone had suddenly caught up with her and had her instantly looking back – cavorting up and down the slopes of grass with her friend with little more on her mind than clambering her way once more to the top.

'Look....You've got to remember I hardly know you,' she said.

She looked down. She was rocking herself back and forth, her arms still hunched around drawn-up knees.

Oggie – quick to read the situation – was equally quick to set her mind at rest.

He tilted her face towards him. For a moment she hesitated, as if weighing the implications of her next move. And then – her hand rising to his shoulder – she relented, and he was awarded the first kiss, their faces slightly angled.

Several knolls away, Digga and Tracy were seated with knees drawn to their haunches. She had been counting his eye-lashes which were amazingly long, like spiders' legs. She had a thing about eye-lashes. She also had the feeling that Digga was shy, which, if anything, she thought was quite cute. Maybe if she were to lie back in the grass. She leant back, ready to assume control, pulling him towards her. Feeling like one of those puppets dangling on a string, he leant to meet her.

Hayley had allowed Oggie's hand to find its way to her left breast where it remained a while, kneading and probing. Only when it made a play for her top button, did she reach across, halting him in his tracks. He retracted, and for a while contented himself with a further exploration of her top, whilst leaning across, eager to reassure her that he liked her and had no intention of doing anything untoward. She explained that she liked him too, but pointed out there was no need to rush things, particularly as they'd only recently met. Plus – and he may as well know this – she wasn't on the pill...she didn't use anything else....and she didn't allow condoms as she didn't trust them.

Oggie reached for his cigarettes.

Digga had kissed Tracy about half a dozen times. He liked kissing her and she liked kissing him too and as a consequence, had allowed his hand – under her supervision – to drop from her shoulder to her left breast, where, for some time, it had remained, his fingers making tiny circles around and across the tips. After which, she kissed him again and pulled him down deeper into the bed of grass.

After a little soul-searching, Hayley had allowed the buttons of her blouse to be undone and the flaps parted. Oggie, having perused the bra-cups, was engaging in a little spider tickling across her tummy to a point just beneath her left rib-cage, making her giggle and roll from side to side: actions which – coupled with the exposed bra and flailing blouse – excited him considerably, prompting him to reach for the left cup which he hoiked up, revealing the first of the two raspberry-tipped mounds.

He nudged a finger against the belt of her jeans. She caught his eye and looked down.

Digga and Tracy had been taking it in turns to lie, fully clothed, on top of each other: one – a soldier, the other – a captive, taking turns to force each other into states of submission. It was Digga's turn. Pinned underneath him, he knew she was powerless to avoid him – her giggling confirmed the fact – as did the wet raspberry kisses he was depositing on her forehead and the feel of his nose sliding back and forth across hers. He was in control, and as if to prove the point, dipped his head, this time to bite the lobe of her left ear.

They had come to a sort of arrangement – or Hayley had. In fulfilling her part in the deal, she had released the belt and the clasp of her jeans and hitched them down beneath her buttocks, snicking her knickers in the process, as Oggie watched on from the side. That done, she eased the panties down off her hips. Oggie snuffed the cigarette out in the grass.

Tracy had been showing Digga how to play lizard-heads with the tips of their tongues and then allowed him to knead her breast through the blouse with rhythmic tweaks of his fingers, like a child with a toy hooter. As reward for his efforts, she leant across him and kissed him – open mouthed.

It was after a period of exploratory fondling that Oggie found himself gazing at the fleshy orifice.

'There,' breathed Hayley. 'Just there.'

He looked to where her finger was stabbing at the strange pimply thing winking at him from the top of her crack.
'Where?' he said.
'There...' she said, her breath coming in a series of quick gasps. 'Just there.'
Oggie watched as she attempted to negotiate his finger somewhere along the line of slippery wrinkles.
It was peachy and wet – his finger suddenly disappearing somewhere inside.
'There!'
'What?'
He made a play to kiss her, but her lips seemed to have disappeared somewhere over her left shoulder.

He watched again as she reached down, substituting her own finger and spearing it into the splayed flesh, her breath coming in quick bursts.
'What?'

Seconds later the girl was lost to the fuzziness of a rapidly moving hand and the urgent pounding of her right buttock – humping and bumping – effectively thrusting him aside, back to his former position – where he was suddenly overcome with the urge to start slapping her tits with forward and backward swings of his right hand.

Hayley twisted and shifted herself this way and that, strange cackling noises emanating from the base of her throat. Until – almost as swiftly as it had started – she was back in the grass, lying flat and wheezing gently. She sighed and lay still, narrow eyes peeping up from semi-closed eyelids.

Oggie, sensing a need to keep his distance, was back on his haunches, looking out across the adjacent hillocks. And then back to the sight of her knickers being hoisted into place along her thighs.

He watched as she drew the sides of her blouse together and began the buttoning process.
'What?' he said again, convinced something had happened but at a loss as to what it could be.

'Nothing,' she said. 'Don't worry about it.'

She made a move to sit up, but Oggie, sensing the need to take a firm hand, laid a few fingers against her, pressing her back, a hand pushing repeatedly into the ball of her shoulder.

Her voice was at once relaxed, almost placatory.

'It's alright....leave it,' she said, though less convincing now, and making a deliberate play of brushing grass off the arms of her blouse.

Oggie was immediately on his feet – stepping back to observe the debacle shaping up beneath him.

'What's your fuckin' problem?' he said, a foot nudging at her, pawing at her. She was the one who'd asked *him* out, maybe she'd forgotten that.

She recoiled and turned away, her face buried in a clump of grass.

He looked across the neighbouring dunes and then looked down. With a final disparaging kick – he was off, careering over the nearest of them – peering into the distance.

Digga and Tracy – in the midst of their latest and most ardent clinch – were aware of plodding feet and muffled shouts.

Seconds later, Oggie was stood above them, his eye flitting from behind to the pair rolling merrily in the grass beneath him.

'Come on, we're goin',' he announced, thumping a fist repeatedly into the palm of his hand. He looked back.

Tracy and Digga exchanged glances, Digga drawing himself away, Tracy looking anxiously toward the top of the grassy verge.

At the top of the knoll Digga – still struggling with his shirt – looked back.

'See you tomorrow,' he said, catching Tracy's parting look.

She nodded and stood, straightening her blouse in silence before making her way back along the grassy path.

Oggie's attentions were set firmly in the opposite direction. 'Come on,' he said again – renewed impatience at his friend's dithering. He stopped for a final look over his shoulder.

'What a stupid bitch.'
Digga, having scrambled his way across the clumps of grass, looked back with him.
'What?'
    Digga scoured the scene for a parting glimpse of Tracy.
'Birds...' said Oggie.
'What was it.....hormones?' asked Digga, still staring at the last of the grassy knolls.
'Fuckin' hormones or what?' said Oggie, already on his heels and urging Digga to get a move on.

Maurice's Wedding Night

One day there were four boys to be seen shepherding another boy – a big lethargic-looking boy, with jam-jar spectacles – off the road and onto a path that led into a quiet stretch of woodland.

The leader of the boys – Hook, 'H' to close friends – was in pole-position. He was a tall lean-looking boy with a shock of black hair and thin piercing eyes.

At his side was Splinter – a kind of lieutenant – similarly built and carrying a haversack of tools on his back. He rarely said much when they were on a mission. His job was to keep an eye to their right, guarding against prying eyes.

Blimp was the third member of the crew. By contrast, a rotund, squat individual with short stumpy legs. His job was to keep an eye to the left, where there were fewer trees – watching for onlookers peering from their washing-lines or the houses that bordered the path.

The fourth member of the 'crew' was a boy called SIT – 'Say It Twice' – a boy with a strange and at times frustrating habit of repeating himself – and others – and at often, quite inopportune moments.

There was also a fifth boy present. Simon was the youngest – a recruit – a quiet contemplative boy found wandering the sands near Blackpool, and brought into the 'fold' some four weeks ago. He was a bright boy and to all intents and purposes, was Hook's protégé, though as contrasting in appearance as was possible: slight and fair-haired as opposed to Hook's lean, hawk-like look.

Simon's role was simple – to watch and learn. It was his third mission and he was still learning the ropes and trying to get the hang of things.

The boy they were ushering along the path was called Maurice – Maurice Batt. He was without doubt one of life's sad cases: grossly overweight, bespectacled to a point of near-blindness and, as a consequence, almost universally despised (or when he was lucky, ignored). Some said he had a hair-lip too. He was also somewhat slow-witted: the kind who permanently hover on the brink of things, whilst deluding themselves – and seeking to delude others – that they're 'in on the action'.

The boys were shepherding Maurice to a quiet spot midst surrounding trees and a tumbling stream. They were taking him there to be married. He was going to marry every schoolboy's raven-haired, hazel-eyed pin-up beauty – Melanie Munro.

'How much further?' asked Blimp, whose miniscule legs were beginning to scratch and scrape against the increasingly irritating bramble.

No-one bothered answering him. His complaints, largely brought about by his stumpy appearance, were commonplace. And in any case, it didn't really make much difference how much further.

Rather than taking Maurice to be married, they were taking him to be laid down in a clearing in the woods where he would be tethered to four trees with rope.

'Ain't much further,' announced SIT – pointing the way ahead. 'Few yards,' he said nodding at a clump of trees ahead. 'Few yards this way.'

No-one said anything.

Blimp had torn a twig off a tree and was brandishing it as if to beat off unwanted predators.

Maurice was content to amble along in the boys' shadow. The clearing they were heading for couldn't be much further. And once there – or soon after – he was going to marry Melanie Munro. He would be tied down in the grass beforehand – it was all part of the arrangement, a private arrangement. Splinter was already in the process of lowering the bag from his shoulder. Simon was watching quietly from the rear.

It was about a minute later that they arrived at the clearing – a quiet spot with four trees placed equidistant midst a nest of bushes and a tumbling stream. Blimp went to the stream and leant down to drink from its tiny pools in the bend. Hook told him not to be so stupid as the water was still and therefore could be infected and poisonous. He abandoned the idea and returned to his place.

Attention was immediately on Maurice, around whom they had gathered in a sort of semi-circle. Splinter had the haversack in his left hand.

Hook took a few steps forward and looked Maurice in the eye. 'Maurice – what is it you want more than anything?' he asked.

Maurice stared vacantly at the trees, pointedly avoiding all their gazes.

'To be tethered to the ground – to the four trees,' he said, nodding at the four trees or branches of trees expediently placed around them.

'What for?' asked Blimp.

Hook gave him 'the eye' and then shifted his gaze back to Maurice.

Hook signalled to Splinter to start extracting the ropes.

'Explain...' said Hook, returning his attention to Maurice.

Maurice stared into space; the jam-jar specs misting up in the increasing chill of late afternoon.

'I mean to show the world that I'm a survivor,' he said.

'A survivor?' queried Hook, eyeing the others before returning his attention to Maurice

'Yes. I wish to spend the night tied down and spread-eagled in the grass. I wish to show the world that I'm a survivor – that I can survive out here – in the dark.....'

Splinter peered at the boy, turned and spat on the ground.

'How will anyone know?' he said, 'that you have survived the night?'

Maurice looked at him.

'If one of you would come to release me in the morning, then *you'd* know,' he said.

Splinter, Blimp and SIT exchanged looks. Then looked across at Hook, who was looking straight at Maurice.

'That will be no problem,' he said, looking him in the eye. 'If that's what you want.'

Maurice had barely moved an inch and was still staring into space.

Blimp reached down to scratch his calves. It was getting chilly and the gnats were beginning to bite. He was wishing they'd get a move on.

Maurice had been telling fibs. He had neither the desire nor the intention of being tied to four trees overnight. He simply wanted to be tied down for a short while, in order to be married.

Hook had been telling lies too.

Glances at watches confirmed that time was getting on. It was down to Splinter, being the lieutenant, to oversee the bonding procedure.

Stepping forwards, he urged Maurice to lower his flabbiness to the ground and spread it – crucifix-style – in the grass.

The others closed in to get a better view. Except SIT who Hook told to remain on the periphery to keep an eye out for outsiders.

Maurice was more than happy to be tied to four trees. It meant that his wedding was imminent.

Having spread himself in the grass, he extended his arms – allowing Splinter to tie each to a nearby tree or one of its stout branches with a length of rope. With his arms tied he was completely helpless.

Splinter turned his attention to his feet, pulling each leg in the direction of the two remaining trees. The other boys were following proceedings closely, but from a safe distance. Simon too was watching carefully, occasionally flipping a wad of blond hair from his eyes.

Minutes later it was done: Maurice was spread-eagled in the grass – completely and utterly helpless. It occurred to Splinter that were they to gather round and kick him to death, there would be little to stand in their way and no-one would know a thing about it.

Each of the boys took their turn, giving him the *look* whilst saying nothing. Splinter had replaced the tools in his haversack and was keeping a close eye on Hook, in anticipation of the next move. 'All clear?' said Hook, looking beyond their heads to check no strangers had seen fit to venture anywhere near the scene. A few heads nodded in confirmation.

'Right,' he said. 'Let's go....'

They turned to leave, heading in the direction of the stream. Hook was the last. He cast a parting glance at the figure lying star-fish style in the grass.

'See you in the morning, Maurice,' he said, before turning to join the others.

There would have been some surprise had the others heard him use his name. Maurice strained his neck to look up from the grass and nodded. Simon too gave Maurice a parting glance and, fleetingly, their eyes met. He looked away and fell quickly into line with the others, not wishing to be seen dithering.

Maurice was pleased that the boys had gone. It meant his dreams of a wedding were close to becoming a reality. He knew this because the note: the 'missive' from his girlfriend had said so and he had followed instructions down to the finest detail. He settled back, content to watch the clouds scuttle across the sky and to listen to the pitter-patter of the nearby stream.

He had found the note hidden in the heel of his trainers in the cloakroom at school. It was the last of three notes: each – hand-written – from Melanie Munro herself...

Not surprisingly, the first was the one that would remain forever etched in his memory – the one he had found sellotaped to his desk one morning before registration.....

...*MM4MB......Maur 4 Mel......Maur 4 Me – 4ever –* signed *MM......*
PS...*don't you DARE tell anyone...not ever!*

This would remain with him because all he normally got from girls – and the boys – was that they either blanked him or bombarded him with abuse.

Despite immediately falling in love with Melanie Munro, he knew that girls liked to have their secrets. Like the second note he had found the following day taped to his sports-bag in the cloakroom.

Maur... I love you......but......if you tell anyone...I will hate you......always.
And...Remember......You must never speak to me or come near me or look at me...until THE moment...... when we will be together...luv you lots......MM......
PS......instructions re latter, to follow shortly...XXX

Maurice liked the second note almost more than the first because it was the one that made it *official*. *Her* secret had become *his* secret; and now it was *both* their secret. And – there was more to come; he knew that because the letter had said so......

The boys had traipsed their way back along the path. Blimp, holding up the rear, was tiring. His short stumpy legs were doing twice as much work as the others. He explained his problem but no-one seemed to care, or to be listening.
'That's it – job done,' said SIT, brandishing a stick at a nearby bush. 'Done and dusted.' No-one was listening to him either.

Once back on the road, they stamped mud and grass off their shoes and sought to bring some warmth back to their fingers. Evening was drawing in and there was a distinct chill in the air.

It was a short distance along the road that another path led off to the right – a tarmac path this time, taking them over the stream and into the lower corner of Hook's crescent. Hook led them along the path to a pedestrian crossing and then across to a café on the corner.

He looked at his watch. And then ushered each of them into the café where they took their seats and ate cake and drank coke as Hook regaled them with accounts of past conquests, and Splinter chipped in with a few of his own recollections.

It was some time later that Hook made his way to the door and stepped outside.

Though fading, the light was still high enough, its shadows of lamps and houses stretching the full curve of the street ahead.

He stamped his feet and casting an eye towards the heavens, signalled the others to get up and join him.

They knew the route, but still followed Hook, who led them along the avenue away from the café, then second left and first right. A fence at the end indicated the beginning of the woods.

Hook's house was a rambling four storey building with a communal entrance and separate doorways leading off three flights of stairs. They all felt more than at-home here, except for Simon, who was still learning the ropes and had only been here twice. He actually found the place a bit scary.

Having hiked their way up the stairs with the obligatory protests from Blimp, they waited for Hook to unlock the door and then followed him into a spacious, though near-empty room: a sofa angled in one corner, an empty fireplace stuck at the side. The lights remained off.

Dominating the room was a huge curtainless window, offering splendid views across the woods and beyond. The boys lined themselves behind Hook, who opened a drawer to reach for a pair of binoculars, a legacy of his late grandfather.

Surrounded by expectant faces, he raised the binoculars to his eyes and peered across the trees, making minor adjustments to the wheel. And then stopped and grinned. The others grinned too – though as yet, only guessing what it was they were grinning at.

Without uttering a word, Hook handed the binoculars to Splinter and indicated a point beyond a clump of trees to the left. Splinter raised the glasses and immediately the grin broadened. The others followed suit and gave each other looks and patted each other on the back.

It was Blimp's turn next, though he had to stand on a chair to see. Then SIT.

Before long the grins had escalated to a collective-chuckle. And within the minute, all the boys were laughing. And grabbing at each other to reclaim the binoculars from each others' possession. Simon too was smiling. He'd had a look, though not entirely sure, at first, what he was supposed to be looking at. He wasn't overly surprised when he found out.

Hook allowed time for the laughter to wane, before reclaiming the glasses for a more leisurely perusal of the figure who appeared not to have moved an inch.

Maurice hadn't moved an inch because he was still tied to the trees and consequently incapable of doing anything, other than lie there, freezing, wondering how much longer it would be before he was married.

For several minutes the glasses continued to be passed round, though soon more from routine as any source of amusement. Each knew there was little more to see and that little was likely to change. Maurice would remain – tied to the four trees, possibly – throughout the night – maybe even beyond.

It was only after a last round of viewing that Hook reclaimed the binoculars for a final look.

Moments later, he lowered the glasses and stared out into the night. The room fell silent.

'Stupid prick,' he said reaching for the case and flicking open its lid. He wasn't laughing anymore. And interestingly, neither was anyone else. Splinter drew to his side.

There was a uniformed nodding of heads before he turned to the chest of drawers at their side.

'Come on H....read the note,' said Splinter. 'The third one.' He was almost laughing again in anticipation.

Hook went to the top drawer and removed a photocopied piece of A4 paper.

'SIT...hit the light,' he said, unfolding the paper. Splinter and Blimp closed in as SIT made for the switch and the room was suddenly bathed in orange light.

Hook flicked the paper, preparing to speak. No-one else spoke.

Darling......Although I love you, as yet I know not of your love for me......

He ignored the titters, and read on. It was on completion of the reading culminating in the....

Luv u Lots xxxx...M4M...CU Saturday...

PS: use a space between four trees about twenty feet from the tumbling stream xxx
that a round of applause and a few whoops and hollers broke out. Hook lowered the paper, satisfied that all seemed to be in order.

'What a prick,' said Splinter.

'What a wanker,' said Blimp.

'What a wanker,' said SIT. 'A complete and utter wanker.'

Ignoring the air of hilarity Hook walked to the window. The glasses would remain in the drawer. He had no further use of them. And in any case, the light was fading, the possibility of further viewing rapidly rescinding.

Simon shifted from his place at the rear to stand beside Hook. Aware of his presence, Hook looked down.

'Okay?'

Simon nodded, never sure whether Hook's greetings were an invitation to speak or a reminder to look and keep his mouth shut. Hook nodded in the direction of the woods.

'He's a prick,' he said. 'But – we're doing him a favour. You *do* see that don't you?'

Simon nodded again. He sort of saw it. Or at least sought to convey the impression he did. Hook saved him having to agonise over it for too long.

'We're teaching him a lesson,' he said finally, turning to the scene beyond the garden fence. To *think*..... To use this.'

Turning, he made a playful grab for Simon's neck, curling an arm round his shoulder and rapping a knuckle lightly against his blond quaff. And then promptly releasing him, checking to see whether he had anything to say on the subject.

Simon had heard the line on two previous occasions – both from the same vantage point – standing right there, staring out of the window. He knew too that there were times to speak and times when it's best to say nothing. For the moment, at least, he thought it best to say nothing.

Behind them, phase two of the evening was set to get underway.

Drawing two boxes and laying a board across to make a rough and ready table, the boys settled themselves for the next stage of proceedings. Hook drew a pack of cards from the side and began to shuffle the pack to deal a hand to each in turn.

Simon watched on, unsure whether he was to be considered as a later contender. Only when Hook drew another stool and tapped it as invitation to join them, did he become the fifth member of the circle. But then, only to watch and observe.

The games were simple: games of luck and chance – 'Match And Shout', 'Chase The Ace'......'Diamonds High' Then later, the more intricate.... 'Hunt the King', 'One In, Two Out' and finally, to end the evening in style, a few rounds of Poker, each conspiring to throw Blimp and SIT into states of sublime confusion.

Simon played his part. His role was to look and to learn – to pick up the patterns of play; to follow the wheeling and dealing in Hook's more experienced hand – learning the various strategies – particularly in the later rounds.

It was some time later that the crew assembled at the window one last time.

By now the moon was high; its silvery sheen already lacing the lamps and curve of trees beyond the fence. There was little more to see, or to be said; as SIT had aptly put it, all was done and dusted. With a few yawns from Blimp, they made for the door.

Last to leave the scene – Simon allowing his eye to drift once more across the trees before turning to the table and the pack of cards being replaced in the top drawer.

Back in the clearing in the woods Maurice had never been so cold. The only times he'd imagined such temperatures were when he'd contemplated hiding in the freezer to escape his grandmother's scaldings. As well as cold, he was confused.

He was sure he'd got it right. It had seemed a strange thing to do, but he'd heard that girls sometimes liked you to do strange things, and it *was* Melanie Munro. He'd gone over the instructions several times in his room at home, working along each line with his finger: what he should tell the boys, and why – that they would be happy to tie him to four trees, which – when she arrived on the scene to find him waiting for her – spread-eagled on the ground tied to four trees – would…'*like…drive her crazy…?*' At which point she would release him, and they would be married.

But maybe he'd got it wrong. It wouldn't be the first time, nor the last. Or maybe something had happened. Maybe she was ill or got waylaid in the bushes by madmen. Already, a dull pain had worked its way from his extremities to both hips and shoulders. He'd tried pulling on the ropes but they'd remained firmly attached to the trees. He'd tried calling out – calling her name – or anyone – someone out walking their dog or lovers out for a moonlight stroll. But to no avail; that night – it seemed – the woods were his alone.

It was as he was manoeuvring his fingers in an attempt to restore some sense of feeling, that he heard a strange rustling from somewhere over by the stream.

He tried raising himself but a sharp pain across his neck and shoulders drew him back. He managed to crane his neck at an angle of something like forty degrees.

The noise grew to the unmistakeable treading of feet. And then – a figure semi-silhouetted against the moon – crouching at his side, foraging at something in the earth.

'Melanie?'

'Shhhh.'

The warning came suddenly and was followed by a scurrying in the grass.

'What _____'

'Shhhh.' It was followed by a face reaching across – a kid's face.

He was ordered to keep quiet and wait a moment.

He could see a boy – it was certainly a boy – working at the first of the knots.

Like a stuck pig, he lay there, wondering what was going on. There was something about the boy that was familiar. Maybe a boy from school.

'I was here earlier,' the boy muttered, drawing the first rope from Maurice's left wrist and reaching across for the second.

Maurice blinked and drew his numbed arm to his side. He tried looking up again.

The instructions were repeated, to keep quiet and lie still, as the second rope was drawn from his wrist. Maurice obliged on both counts.

Seconds later, the remaining ropes were untied and Simon shuffled across to ditch them somewhere behind a tree.

From his vantage point on the fringe of the clearing, he stood and watched as Maurice began the business of hauling himself to his feet – observing the painful process of restoring himself to a semi-upright position, clinging to a tree and fumbling around with his glasses, trying to re-align them on the bridge of his nose.

He allowed him a few seconds to complete his wheezing and fumbling around with his spectacles, and then stepped across making a grab for his arm, leading him across the clearing, like a child with a handicapped relative.

'We need to go,' he said.

With a parting glance behind, Maurice allowed himself to be led down to where the path worked its way alongside the stream.

Simon steadied him, and then released him, watching him plod his way along the narrow path, looking with each step, as if he might keel over and disappear in the undergrowth. But he needed to do these things for himself, there was little point in anyone stepping in and doing it for him.

He had one eye on his watch and the other on the line of buildings, visible only as a dark shadow silhouetted to a curve on the far side of the fence. A few lights were on but he had no means of identifying exactly where.

Once beyond the worst of the undergrowth the path had them back on familiar territory. Simon's pace quickened, his demand on Maurice unrelenting.

It was as they approached the fence that Maurice stopped, finally able to catch his breath and take stock of events. He looked across the narrow path.

'Thanks,' he said.

Simon nodded, urging Maurice to keep moving and keep his eye on the path.

It was once back on the road that a halo of light from the street-lamp finally jogged Maurice's memory.

'I remember you,' he said, seeing Simon for the first time and then quickly looking at the ground and shuffling his foot against the kerb...'From earlier.'

Simon was already contemplating his next move – beyond the fence running alongside the path opposite. He stopped and looked to where Maurice's moonlike face remained semi-illuminated under the street lamp.

'Where's Melanie?' Maurice asked, head-bowed. Simon thought for a moment before he answered.

'Forget Melanie Munro....' he said. 'It's just a game....They're playing games...'

Maurice watched him step towards the kerb.

'Where you from?' he asked suddenly. There was something about the boy's voice that sounded vaguely familiar.

Simon stopped short of the kerb and looked back.

'Blackpool,' he said.

Maurice stared.

'I went to Blackpool with my uncle and Aunty Gwyneth when I was little,' he said. 'We stayed in a caravan.'

Simon appeared not to hear, or not to be listening. There was a point beyond the fence where the path picked up its route toward the far corner of the field. He stepped towards it.

'They went to live there. But they don't live together any more,' he said. 'I don't know where they live now.'

Maurice's jam-jar spectacles had misted up and he was having trouble focusing as Simon crossed the road and climbed over the stile that would drop him on the path to the next field. 'I haven't seen them for years,' he said finally, before turning to make his way along the road.

Collington Station – Sparrow-Farts

At five-o-four am during the winter months daylight is yet to break over Collington station. There is only an inky-blue sky dotted with stars.

At five-o-five steps approached the ramp-walkway and ventured onto Platform One: the platform for trains to Eastbourne, Brighton and London. The steps were those of Gerald Forskett, and once on the platform he looked up and down the line for any signs of activity. There were none. He looked at his watch. The train would likely be somewhere round Hastings.

At this time of the morning there is rarely much activity on either platform – Platform One or Platform Two: the platform for St. Leonards, Hastings and Ore. No-one was waiting on Platform Two.

It was decidedly chilly. Gerald stamped his feet in small circles in an attempt to keep the chill out.

Moments later, footsteps approached the platform. Gerald looked round to see Dave, hands in pockets, stride onto the platform and look casually down the line.

'Dave.' It was his customary greeting and he watched him nod and take his place at the front of the platform, glancing at his watch.

'No Carol yet?' said Dave, looking up.

'Not yet,' said Gerald, looking to the entrance behind. 'She'll be along soon I expect.'

He looked up and down the line. 'So, where are we Dave?

Dave checked with his watch.

'Five-o-eight...' He was eyeing the movements of the second hand.

'About to enter Hastings tunnel,' he said, sounding much like a station-announcer and looking up.

Gerald breathed into his cupped his hand. He was looking in the other direction towards Cooden Beach. There was little happening in that direction either. There was the sound of footsteps and seconds later, Carol – looking resplendent as ever in a long cherry-red coat and carrying a black leather handbag – emerged on the platform wearing a smile.

'Hi....' She huddled closer, stepping out of the chill and looking at the pair of them. She was breathing into her cupped fists and tapping both against her collar.

'Chilly this morning. Hi Dave.'

Dave moved closer. 'Hi.'

'Hope it's on time,' said Carol, looking along the line.

'It will be,' said Dave, looking at his watch. 'Already pulling into St. Leonards.' he said. 'Actually *in* the station now.' He looked at Carol.

Gerald chuckled.

'So....How's Carol? Did you get that business sorted?'

Carol winced and rolled her eyes.

'I'll tell you about it later...Yes – finally.'

She had opened her handbag and was searching for something in the rear section. She had her keys in one hand. She seemed to be struggling to find whatever it was she was looking for.

Gerald and Dave watched her, but only briefly.

'Just checking I've got the letter,' she said, without looking up.

'It'll be there somewhere,' said Dave.

'It's bloody cold, I know that much,' Gerald said, hands in pockets and stepping in brisk circles.

It *was* cold. And the moon, clear as a bell in the empty sky was indication it seemed set to remain so.

Carol closed her handbag.

'It's there. I knew it was, but I just wanted to be sure.'

'I'm like that,' said Gerald. 'With me it's keys.' He stamped his feet and looked up at Orion, looking particularly lord-like in the star-struck heavens. 'Orion's looking a bit lively this morning,' he said.

'Often does this time of year,' said Dave, looking up.

'And the moon looks beautiful,' said Carol looking to the sky beyond the cone of Beachy Head.

Eyes followed her gaze. Gerald was peering down the line.

'Update me Dave?' he said.

Dave looked at his watch.

'Five eleven….All carriages currently in the tunnel.'

'So you reckon it's on time then.'

'Yep.'

Carol slung the handbag back over her shoulder.

'I'm knackered,' she said with a sigh. 'Someone'll have to kick me to keep me awake.'

'Dave'll kick you,' said Gerald.

Dave had stepped back to pull his coat tighter against a breeze that seemed to have found its way up the ramp and onto the platform. Gerald was looking at his watch.

'Better be on time. I can do without hanging around in this blessed cold any longer than I have to.' He was stamping his feet in an attempt to keep out the chill.

'It will be,' said Dave, looking across for any sign of activity on Platform Two.

Gerald offered to hold Carol's bag whilst she reached for a tissue.

'It's colder than yesterday,' he said, speaking to Dave.

Dave nodded.

Carol blew hard into the tissue, folded it, wrinkled her nose, and offered a quick apology.

At that moment footsteps approached.

It was a man in a thick sheepskin coat who pressed the button for information and then made his way towards the end of the platform where he proceeded to pace up and down.

Dave and Carol observed him for a moment, as did Gerald who looked back and then looked at his watch.

'Update me Dave?' said Gerald.

'Just about to pick up speed; the first three carriages passing the junction,' said Dave, looking at his watch. Gerald chuckled and clamped his arms round his waist.

'You slay me Dave. Did you hear that?' he said, speaking to Carol. He looked along the platform to where a single light illuminated the automatic ticket-machine. Behind which, trees stood silhouetted, swaying their own macabre-like dance to the early-morning breeze.

'So – optimistic?' Gerald turned to Carol.

'Yeh...mostly,' she said.

'It'll be fine,' said Gerald reassuringly.

Something stirred in Dave's pocket and they watched as he took a step backwards and took out his blackberry and peered into it.

'Don't you worry,' said Gerald speaking to Carol.

'Bartholomews,' Dave said, looking up, clutching the phone to his ear and taking a few further steps back. Gerald watched him briefly.

Carol did a few quick jogging steps from foot to foot and turned to look down the line. Dave replaced the blackberry and rejoined them.

'Bartholomews – I left a message,' he said.

'Brrrr....I'm freezing,' said Carol. 'They didn't say anything about this wind.'

'They didn't day anything about it being this cold,' said Dave.

'Said it'll get warmer tomorrow.' Gerald pulled his coat tight and looked in the other direction. He looked at his watch.

'You're looking particularly smart today,' said Gerald, speaking to Carol.

'Well....you've got to make the effort,' said Carol.

'Someone's got to,' said Dave. 'Nice shoes.'

'Got them in town,' said Carol, looking down. Gerald looked at his watch.

'Update us Dave?'

'Just pulling into Bexhill station,' said Dave, looking at his watch. 'Approaching the church opposite the station.'

'Hear that Carol?' said Gerald. He looked across to see Carol tottering a bit on her heels in an attempt to keep out the cold. 'Careful now,' he said. She stood still and reached into her handbag.

'Tissue anyone?' There was a shaking of heads.

'No thanks.'

'Not yet,' said Dave, wrinkling his nose and watching the man in the sheepskin coat pacing up and down the end of the platform.

'Hope the heating's on in the train,' said Carol.

'It will be,' said Dave.

'I'm just going to curl up into a ball and fall asleep,' said Carol closing her eyes in anticipation.

'That's your prerogative,' said Gerald. 'I might join you.'

'Not too close,' said Dave, giving them both a warning look. 'This is a family show.'

'Oh I don't know, said Carol shuffling a little closer to Gerald and replacing a tissue in a pocket in her handbag.

Gerald looked down the line.

The announcement came out of the blue from a tiny speaker pinned to one of the stanchions, announcing the approaching train and its stopping points en-route to London. Then the machine clicked off.

Dave looked at his watch. Carol looked in the direction of the approaching train.

Seconds later – a cone of light crept into view along the rails, followed, seconds later, by a line of dimly lit carriages.

Carol stepped back. Gerald stepped to one side to avoid her.

'On time?' he asked, looking at Dave.

'Dead on time,' said Dave, looking at his watch.

Moments later, the train drew to a halt. And a moment after that, Gerald pressed the button and the door slid open.

'After you,' he said, to Carol.

'Thankyou,' said Carol, stepping onto the train.

Dave stepped forwards.

'After you,' said Gerald to Dave.

'Thankyou,' said Dave, following Carol.

Seconds later, Gerald followed them. Moments later, the doors drew shut.

The train began to draw away from Platform Two. The next stop would be Cooden Beach, arriving at five twenty-one.

The Pub Man

Ullte Meerschaum, a tall lean man, clad in black trilby and long sweeping coat and carrying a black executive-style briefcase, paused at a point on the brow of the hill, eyeing the line of terraced cottages, beyond which the road forked round a small traffic island and its medieval stone wall.

It was from a distance of some fifty yards that he first spotted the plaque hanging from its metal frame and, for the time being, at least, that was all he needed to see.

He at once quickened his pace.

It was a fine building, for sure; its stone walls and oakwood surround – a quality of workmanship rarely encountered in the more modern enclaves of the city.

Chin back – he tweaked the collar and reached to adjust the belt around his girth. And looking once more at the tavern sign, unmistakeable in the light of early evening – he made his way to the door.

His arrival brought a jangling from above and a number of eyes turning in his direction.

He stood a moment, settling the trilby more firmly on his head and brushing a few flecks from the spankingly smart coat – aware that his presence was likely set to come under even closer scrutiny.

With a brush of his lapels, he made his way to the bar where the bar-woman – an ageing soul in dirndl and clogs – was quick to place herself at his disposal.

Placing both hands upon the bar, he nodded at the nearest bar-pump.

'A jug of your brewer's best,' he said, making every effort with his city enunciation.

The woman scuttled off, leaving the man to take his place upon the stool and place his case beside it.

Settling into place, he made a point of reminding himself that patience was the name-of-the-game in these places, the consumption of ale being a serious business – a far cry from the 'don't blame me mate I don't drink it' syndrome that was often the case elsewhere.

He watched as the jug was first angled to catch the initial flow, and then steadied and over a period of some three to four minutes, repeatedly levelled with a spatula, allowing space and time for the procedure to be repeated. He watched too, the woman's manner in tending to it, her expression unflinching – as she deftly skimmed the head and placed the jug to one side.

It duly arrived: a fine, full-bodied brew, topped with a snowy head and with a rich aftertaste of malt.

He raised the glass and looked round. The place was beginning to liven up – a few drinkers huddled at tables and in the far alcoves, whilst, at the opposite corner, a fiddler and his piano-accordionist were taking their places on a tiny dais and were in the process of fine-tuning their instruments.

The beer was good, better than he'd imagined, and he already has an eye on its successor, a darker ale brewed over beechwood and with a slight hint of bacon in the aftertaste.

He was ideally perched – a few locals gathered to his right, and to his left – a morose-looking fellow, huge-limbed and wearing a bleak hang-dog expression...

Meerschaum – having clocked the man pretty much since his arrival – acknowledged him briefly, and quickly adopted his posture – arms leaning on the bar, spreading himself in either direction.

His neighbour lit a cigarette. As did Meerschaum. The man drew from the cigarette and broke from his reverie briefly, cocking an eye at a passing punter.

Meerschaum smacked his lips approvingly. It was a good beer, the sharp hoppiness and malty aftertaste already biting deep into his palette – a pint worthy of note.

He took another sip and sneaked a quick glance at his neighbour.

'Good beer,' he said, raising the pot and gazing approvingly into its contents.

The man appeared to have little to say on the subject – wary, no doubt, of launching into half-baked conversations with strangers in pubs, particularly sitting at the bar, and particularly during the earlier, quieter hours of business. He had an eye fixed on the line of bottles opposite, and broke his pose only to reach for his packet of crisps – Roasted Ox – and tear its corner away, taking time out to investigate a few of its contents.

'Good pub too, Meerschaum added, casting an eye over a scene that – even at first glance told its own story: the smattering of drinkers, the brass pumps – ready and waiting at the far end of a bar – lines of trinkets, horse-brasses and just about every other relic of a bygone age dangling endearingly above their heads. And the woman too – perched in her corner, awaiting the ring of the bell to spring her once more into action. All in all – homage to one of the finest and most heralded of traditions: the good old-fashioned, no-nonsense boozer – a tradition Meerschaum was quick to take on-board.

It was as his eye completed its tour, finally resting on the band about to break into their opening reel that he extended an arm.

'Strange to think,' he said, casting a nod at the oak beams and tiny alcoves running off from the corner. 'One day this...The next – some New-Age 'Theme bar' decked out in chrome and swimming in neon lights!'

He tutted visibly and watched as his neighbour seized the crisp-packet and, tilting it by one corner, proceeded to give it a thorough shake above his open mouth, chomping eagerly on its contents. He followed it up by reaching for his jug and hoiking a good third of it down his tube. All of which prompted Meerschaum to follow suit, making a grab for his own glass – eyeing the fuzzy head sticking in long spittle-like streaks to each and every dimple in the glass – always a good sign, or so they say.

He made a point of mirroring the man's movements, also raising pot to mouth, before extending an arm to head height.

'One day this...' he said, tutting even more audibly and levelling the jug – and its nut-brown contents – to public view. 'The next – some yellow concoction, served courtesy of freezing pipes and full of frothy bubbles!'

He made a series of clicking noises, watching, as the man smacked his lips, shuffled on his stool and summoned the woman to order a refill.

Meerschaum, quick to spot his intent, nodded and reached for his wallet: indication that the chap should keep his money in his pocket. The man hesitated, but eventually shoved the glass in his direction. Moments later another two foaming brews stood proudly before them.

'Cheers,' said Meerschaum, raising his glass.

The man grunted – watching a foot extend to nudge the case an inch or two further into the public domain.

There was, at that moment, something of a commotion behind them – 'Party-Time' or so it seemed: a handful of the 'olduns' being frogmarched onto the dance-floor to the tune of embarrassed smiles, cat-calls and foppish owl-like hooting from the flanks. Meerschaum – never one to miss an opportunity – cast a nod in their direction.

'One day – a few old-timers having a knees-up,' he said, gazing wistfully at the whoops and hollers cranking it up from the surrounding tables. 'The next – the whole place, absolutely heavin'. Razor-sharp guys, scanty-clad molls – each and every one of them dripping in gel and with money to burn...'

He sighed and lowered his glass.

The man shuffled the packet and reached lazily for another fistful of its contents.

'Certainly gets you thinking,' Meerschaum said, twirling the glass against the mat and then raising it to dispatch a further third of its contents.

'Cheers,' he said.

The man grunted, shuffling the packet a little more vigorously and then turned, resolved – it seems – to awarding the chap a little closer attention; a brewery-man no doubt: some new-kid-on-the-block sent out to ruffle a few feathers and maybe kick a few backsides, not before time in some cases. He shook the packet and peered contemplatively into its contents.

'Scanty-clad molls huh?' he said, still eyeing the case nudging its way into public view beneath them.

Meerschaum – stealing a quick glance to his left – nodded solemnly.

'You would *not* believe it,' he said. 'So scanty as to be barely worth cladding in the first place.'

'Money to burn huh?'

'Oceans of the stuff,' said Meerschaum. 'Just waiting to be blown on Mickey-Mouse cocktails – sparklers – beach-huts – Christ knows what poking out the glass...You would *not* believe it!'

There was a brief hiatus – the only sound, a rhythmic crunching beneath rotating jaws.

For some moments Meerschaum was neighbour to a man seemingly lost in thought – until finally, a hand extended, beckoning the woman over. Moments later, a brace of cherry liquors sat invitingly on the mat before them.

'Cheers,' said Meerschaum, raising the glass and again following the man's example, downing its contents with a swift flick of the wrist.

The man, having brushed his fingers to remove a smattering of grease and excess crumbs – placed the empty vessel aside for a moment.

'Freezing pipes and frothy bubbles huh...?'

'Absolutely,' says Meerschaum. 'Freezing, frothing, practically foaming over the glass – unbelievable!'

Behind them – the band finally called a halt to their number; opportunity for the 'olduns' to bid a hasty retreat to a tumultuous reception of cat calls and the clatter of glasses on table-tops. All of which served to direct the man's eye once more to the case still stashed securely beneath his neighbour's stool.

He leant lazily on hooked elbows, peering contemplatively into the packet's depths.

'So…you 'ere on business?' he asked.

Meerschaum nodded and took another long hard drink from the jug.

'Pub business,' he said, looking to his left and nodding down at the case. 'And you?'

The man shifted closer – a finger pointing at his chest.

'Me to,' he said, prodding proudly at the mid-point of his breast bone.

'This – is my pub…lock, stock and – *freezing* barrel!'

He sat up, tilting the packet and shaking its corner above his mouth to catch its final residue.

'Really,' says Meerschaum. 'Who would have thought it?' He raised the jug.

'Cheers,' he said.

The man nodded, sucking a few clusters from his teeth and attempting to crunch the cellophane into a tight enough ball to sit comfortably in the ashtray.

'Scanty-clad molls huh?' he said – brushing his hands and smacking his lips.

'Absolutely,' said Meerschaum. 'The whole place – absolutely heaving with them.'

The owner watched as Meerschaum eased the stool back, extended an arm, and drew the executive case onto his lap to release the catches.

'Talking of which___'

He promptly raised the lid.

The pair cast an eye over the glitzy contents: every yard of chrome, every inch of tinsel – all in fully embossed colour and easy to follow, step-by-step instructions. And – thrown in for free, the huge neon sign...*Bubbles*...waiting to be hoisted above the door and displayed in multi-coloured flashing lights.

It was on the stroke of midnight that Meerschaum finally rose from his seat in an adjacent room and, executive case in one hand, shook the hand of his companion with the other.

'G'day to you sir – and to your business – and to your fine drop of ale.'

The man nodded and moments later, reached to snatch the last packet of cashew-nuts from the card, watching as his visitor made his way through the curtain and across the floor to bring a final jingle to the bell above the door.

Seconds later and he was off to the lodgings reserved in his name over the brow of the hill at the top of the street.

It was a month and some days later that Meerschaum found himself once more the brow of the hill eyeing the line of cottages leading down to where the road forked round a small traffic island. Even before he was at the scene the indications were there, confirmed as he took his place before the stone walls.

He was aware too that – at that moment – he was not alone.

A fellow observer – a familiar face, it seemed – stood, hands in pockets, staring glassy-eyed at the scene before them – a morose-looking fellow, faintly bemused and evidently disgruntled at what he was witnessing.

Meerschaum looked on, a wave of conviviality suddenly sweeping over him.

'Alright?' he said, approaching the man in typically bright and breezy fashion.

The man looked up – eyeing the windows, boarded up with plywood – boards nailed across every available space. And then looked across at Meerschaum. He grunted morosely.

'No – I'm not fuckin' well alright,' he said, perusing the metal frame and loose bolts and the sign *Bubbles* leaning against the wall in readiness.

He stepped closer, reading from the sign and then from the rubric pinned to the wall at its side.

'I'm far from fuckin'... *'alright'*,' he said again, staring hard in Meerschaum's direction, as if set to hold him responsible for the state of his disquiet.

Meerschaum moved in, leaning to peer into the one remaining window.

All appeared to be in place: the chrome bars, the tinsel dangling grotto-style beneath displays of flashing lights and alongside lines of plastic beer taps. The sign – *Bubbles* – ready and waiting to be hoisted into place a few yards above their heads.

Meerschaum eyed the man who continued to peruse the scene with the look of a man about to face the executioner's axe.

'I'm away from the place for six fucking weeks, leaving that idle, good-for-nothing, dick-head of a brother in charge – and *this* is what I come home to.'

He turned to face Meerschaum – his expression full of indignation – his eye turning to the oakwood and brick surround – the one remaining edifice of a lifetime's work and ambition.

He looked up and down, leaning to peer dolefully through the remaining window. And looked back, turning swiftly to his left.

'Anyway – who the fuck are you?'

Meerschaum hovered a moment, seeming to take something from the man's moment of disquiet. Taking a firm grip on his case, he moved across, taking a position at the man's side. He sighed and tutted and – urging the man to join him at the window – nudged the hat a little higher on his forehead.

'Picture it...' he said, an arm extending beyond the boarded-up windows to the chrome bars, tinsel and the *Bubbles* sign lying in wait beneath. 'One day – this...'

The other arm reached to the case, drawing it to a firmer grip in his lap.

'The next – a good old-fashioned boozer – selling fine ales – and with nothing to disturb the eye beyond a few 'olduns' having a good old knees-up in the corner_____'

The Issue Of A Lever Being Attached To The Outside Rear Door

On a grey sleepy afternoon in March there was little sign of activity in or around the building, apart from Tom from Flat Five upstairs.

Fancying himself as something of a handyman, Tom was semi-seated in the corridor, a folding-tray toolbox at his side and a scattering of screws, screwdrivers and various other paraphernalia of DIY scattered on the floor around him.

He whistled tunelessly as he worked: drilling, screwing, finally slotting the device into place and securing at with a few further turns of the screwdriver. It was a quick job – and within minutes it was done – a small lever attached to the scratch-plate of the outside door, enabling it to be pulled shut rather than left to close of its own accord.

Whistling a little more melodiously at the job's completion, he packed his tools, and with a quick sweep of the bits and bobs lying around the hallway – he was gone.

On his departure, silence returned and would remain until around six-o-clock when Harold and Jean from Flat Two arrived back from town to find a lever had been attached to the metal plate on the outside door. It hadn't been there when they went out, which meant it must have been attached between eight-thirty and six-o-clock. They leant for a closer look, taking turns to pull at it: first with the door open – then with it shut. Certainly, it hadn't been there when they'd left the property. The logical move was to contact Marilyn in Flat Ten.

Back in their flat, Harold rang Marilyn's number. Marilyn answered the phone and Harold put her in the picture: that a lever had been attached to the rear outside door some time between eight-thirty and six-o-clock. It was vaguely reminiscent of last October when pictures of flying fish had mysteriously appeared on the wall of the communal entrance area.

Marilyn replaced the phone and thought it best to have a look. Harold agreed to pop down and have a look with her.

They arrived at pretty much the same time.

Marilyn looked first, pulling the door open and pushing it shut, then allowing it to close of its own accord, which it just about managed to do. Harold followed suit – with the same result.

It was probably Tom. Tom fancied himself as a bit of a handyman and was in the habit of knocking things up and/or putting things back together. Only last September he'd fixed the lid to the fuse-box and put a new catch on the gas-meter box under the stairs.

They agreed to leave it for now. The following day Marilyn would send a missive round updating everyone on the situation.

The following day the missives went out. She phoned each of the six directors (the residence being a registered Limited Company.) Four were in-residence and arranged to pop down and have a look.

They met in the hallway at eleven and took turns to examine the lever, opening and closing the door, occasionally letting it close of its own accord, which – in all cases – it just about managed to do. It was a solid-looking lever, that much they could agree on.

It was left to Ken from Flat Seven to lay his hands on the appropriate document. It took a while finding it, lying under a pile of Maintenance stuff, AGM minutes and proposals for British Gas's cavity-insulation on all flats in the building. He scanned his eye over the bits relating to *accessibility with reference to communal areas*. It was less than specific on the attachment of levers. The logical move, on consultation with Marilyn, was to hold a meeting in her flat.

Ken phoned Hilary who phoned Edna and then Marilyn who confirmed she'd been thinking along similar lines. She'd get the agendas sorted. The question as to Tom's likely reaction was raised but, as Alice pointed out, you can't exclude people. And Tom might be in a position to enlighten them a little – adding some details of the job...cost etc. Which, of course, assumed Tom *had* been the one to attach the lever. It was generally agreed it had to be Tom – It had *Tom* written all over it.

The agendas went out later that day.

The meeting was held in Marilyn's flat at ten-o-clock the following morning. Tom *wasn't* at the meeting. It began with Harold putting them in the picture: that a lever had been attached to the plate of the rear outside door. It was about one and a half to two inches long and big enough to slip a finger behind to pull the door shut. It had been attached sometime between eleven am. and six-o-clock pm.

Marilyn thanked Harold for that and turned to Ken to update them re the lease, or rules and regulations pertaining to the attachment of things like levers. Ken confirmed that as far as he could ascertain – whilst *levers* weren't stipulated as items per-se, reference was made to maintaining *quick* and *ready* access. Which posed the question: did the lever come under either bracket? Hilary from Flat Eight was of the opinion that it came under *quick,* though Ken pointed out that in official rubric *quick* was often more an 'indicator' than a 'determinator'. *Ready* too wasn't always deemed to be quantifiable.

Which took them to Edna's query as to whether the door would close without the lever. Harold pointed out that it seemed to, but only unofficially – no facts and figures had, as yet, been established.

Hilary volunteered to do a ten minute survey confirming the effectiveness of the door closing without the lever. Marilyn suggested Edna went with her to oversee the procedure.

In their absence the others considered the *appearance* of the lever. It was a sturdy enough lever, there were no dissenters to this, but in other respects, opinions were divided: some claiming it wasn't so pleasing on the eye, that – as levers on doors go – it was a little angular and austere looking, the point being that it would cross their eye each and every time they entered or left the building – by the rear door.

Hilary and Edna were back with the results of the survey. The door closed of its own accord every time but with slight variations of speed (they'd timed the closures using the second hand on Hilary's watch). Conclusion – in a typical day you could reasonably expect the door to close of its own accord. Ken pointed out that the door was designed to close of its own accord and that variations in speed might be due to extraneous circumstances. Hilary made the point that the attachment of a lever might impinge on the door's facility to close pending extraneous circumstances. Which took them back to Marilyn's point.

Edna was a bit confused. Jim, her husband, pointed out they were establishing the implications of a door closing, or not closing, of its own accord – over a finite period –pending extraneous circumstances.

A further potential spanner-in-the-works came from Harold who pointed out that they were discussing the implications of the lever having been fitted with the lever actually attached to the door. But, as the issue was *should* it have been attached, maybe it shouldn't be attached during the course of the meeting, and only attached pending the outcome of the meeting. Hilary pointed that to detach it and attach it made two jobs, whereas to simply detach it would only be one job.

Why complicate matters?

The meeting closed at twelve fifteen with a vote of thanks to all for attending.

After the meeting there was some confusion as to whether they'd decided the lever should or shouldn't have been attached to the door.

But within seconds, it proved to be neither here nor there....

On returning to their side of the building – they discovered the lever had been removed from the door.

There were puzzled expressions and a few tried opening and closing the door without the lever. On all occasions the door closed of its own accord though at varying speeds.

Within seconds Harold was on his mobile. Marilyn answered the phone. Harold put her in the picture – that the lever had been removed.

The question was: *who* could have removed it? They decided it was likely Tom.

Marilyn would send a missive round. They made their way back to their building, none of them noticing the door close behind them.

How To Deal With
A Man's Parting Wish

Montserrat Ethelburgh's four sons sensed something might be afoot when – one fine day they were summoned by local dispatch to make haste to their father's bedside at the local infirmary. Not that they feared the chap was close to dying. For some time, word from the hospital was there was sufficient 'fire in his belly and mischief in his soul' to keep them all on their toes for a while yet, and as such, there seemed no immediate cause for concern.

Yet there was some lively banter as the four made their way along the path that led to the entrance to the hospital. Was it the moment for the family's affairs – or more specifically, their father's affairs – to be laid bare before them? The moment, dare they speculate, for some great family fortune to wind its way into their lap? The youngest, Ezekiel, had thoughts of inheriting the fine gold watch that had been his father's since *his* father's dying day. The eldest, Joshua, having an eye on the hiking boots that had served his father admirably on his treks up and down the mountain, indeed, right up to when his walking days were over and his bed-ridden days had suddenly and inexplicably befallen him some few months previous.

A ring of the bell at their father's door summoned the nurse, who, in turn, escorted them to where their father lay twixt an array of bottles and an arrangement of hooks attached to stands at the bedside in a room so deathly quiet and ghostly as to be almost frozen in time.

But beyond the obvious frailty of the man and the dazzling array of hooks and canisters, a more worrying sight awaited them: their father's head, settled enough on its base of goose-feather pillows, was swathed in white bandages – or rather, the *eyes* were swathed in bandages. There was little by way of movement, no stirring of the neck-muscles, no glancing left or right, a mere blank stare directed at the ceiling as if the enormity of what they were witnessing was yet to fully register with their bearer. Behind the bandage, two thick white wads had been planted firmly over each eye.

The sons were aghast. What was going on? What had happened? Had their father met with some tragic, or semi-tragic, accident? They were of a mind to summon the doctor at once, to have him come and explain the circumstances that had struck their father such a cataclysmic blow.

But, for all *their* shock and concern, there was a measured, almost aloof air in the greeting that urged them take a place at his side and to listen a moment. The chaps placed themselves, two each side of the bed, within close enough earshot to hear his tale: to discover how their father had fallen victim to such a catastrophic turn of events.

He bade them all relax whilst casting an exasperated sigh in the direction of the ceiling. Yes – he had been having problems with his sight. And for some time; and though having failed to make it public knowledge, the facts were plain enough: both eyes had, for some time, been dimming to the point that, at around tea-time the previous Friday, they had finally seen fit to give up the ghost and call it a day. As to *Why*…He threw a questioning arm. Who knows why these things happen? Diet? Hormone deficiencies? Luck of the draw? Of course, it was no mean thing to have to deal with, but at the end of the day these things happen. You look on the bright side – think about those less fortunate than yourself and count your chickens that at least the remainder of the tackle is in reasonable working order. He slapped an emphatic arm on the concrete-hard mattress.

The sons were numb. Forget diet – and hormone deficiencies. What did the doctors have to say? A man doesn't suddenly wake to find he's lost his sight as he might wake to discover he's mislaid his wallet. But their father would have little more said on the matter. Doctors... Pah! What the devil did they know? And promptly turned his head to curtail any further discussion.

But the lads were far from convinced. There was more to hand here than twists-of-fate or deficiencies – of any description; something was afoot. For never had they seen such a dramatic turn-about in a man: one minute skipping gaily en-route to his favourite boozer, the next – pinned to a hospital bed surrounded by more bottles as might be encountered at the doctors' Christmas party! All by 'private arrangement' by all account – another first for the family. They gazed at the lacklustre expression half-hidden behind swathes of bandages.

But first things first. Their immediate concern was here and now. Was there anything *they* could do to ease the pain that – if not literally – he must be suffering in his attempt to come to terms with such a cataclysmic turn of events?

The offer was well received and seemed to stir their father to a degree. Evidently gratified to hear their concern, he drew his sons closer. As it happened there *was* one little favour that might – if not ease the pain – at least bring some consolation: a little respite to what had unquestionably become a somewhat bleak and desultory existence.

The sons were all ears. Anything they could do to ease their father's plight they would surely do.....

Good lads. It was exactly what their father wished to hear.

Propping himself up on one elbow and in a voice that struggled to find space in such claustrophobic surroundings, he had them turn their eye beyond the hospital grounds to a familiar point beyond the low-lying fields – not quite within vision from where they were seated due to two lines of elm trees bordering the hospital grounds.

An exchange of looks confirmed what had likely triggered their father's imagination ...The Mountain!

Perched at the end of the valley like some giant Buddha seated at the head of the family table, The Mountain had – since time immemorial – been the embodiment of everything good and wholesome to the people both in and beyond the valley: the one unshakeable feature in an increasingly unstable world and a source of inspiration to all who lived in its shadow.

And, like all kids raised in the valley, his childhood had been spent exploring its lower slopes, breathing its air and taking in its breathtaking scenery; and, in later years – the tarns and crags leading to the Great Ridge and the great winding path that took all prepared to tread its wild and rocky route to that most magical spot of all – The Summit! A place where time itself seemed to stand still; where a man could be at one with his Maker – the Great Glinting Ocean peering up from the depths beneath.

Yet, for all its place in their people's hearts, here he was – lying bed-bound, several miles away, surrounded by little more than a few prissy lawns, a few lines of daffodils and rows of regimented-looking trees!

So – the answer was 'yes'; there was something they could do. A task that might, at least, ease the pain and bring a little solace to whatever days remained, however numbered they may be…

Silencing their protests he turned again in the direction beyond the hospital grounds.

His wish was that he be taken – albeit 'carried' – just one more time – along the mountain path from the lower slopes to the crags and quarries of the upper slopes and finally to The Summit itself, that he might take in its sweet aromas, the Sea-Of Cairns peering down on the Great Glinting Ocean – just one more time!

At which point he laid his head upon the pillow and turned his unseeing-stare once more upon the ceiling.

The sons looked at each other blankly. Beloved father or not – what they were witnessing were the rantings of a man who had clearly lost his senses along with his sight. To lead the chap by the hand would be task enough, to *carry* him – along the path to the wild rocky slopes of the mountain's summit – on a stretcher – would be well nigh impossible.

It was a conundrum none of them had bargained for. Nor one that appeared to have any quick or easy solution. To deny their father a parting wish, and as such, be seen to be failing in their duty as devoted sons? Such a scenario was near as unthinkable as the business of getting him up the mountain in the first place – wherein lay the rub!

It was following much scratching of heads and exchanging of glances, that the middle son – Jeremiah – whose knowledge of the mountain was second to none and who perhaps had the edge on the others when it came to adopting a more practical approach to these things – ushered the others to one side.

He drew them to a huddle. They would need to listen – and listen carefully. There *was* a solution; one that – whilst maybe ruffling a few feathers – would certainly go some way to ticking all the required boxes!

There were blank looks and puzzled expressions. The brother drew a warning finger across his lips, a reminder that what he was about to say must remain strictly between the four of them.

The solution was that they *would* oblige their father in his one remaining wish – or – at least, be *seen* to 'oblige' him.

He drew an arm across their shoulders, drawing them closer, urging them to take heed.

Their father's senses were gone – so much was obvious. His eyesight too was shot to pieces – and his legs, for some reason, had seen fit to follow suit. He broke off a moment, checking that their father – or what remained of him – was still beyond earshot before continuing.

If a little of the mountain air was what the man desired, then a little of the mountain air he shall have. For whilst schlepping the guy to the summit was a non-starter, what would he know of how close, or distant, they were from it? Were they to simply hover up and down on the spot all day long, who'd be any the wiser? Certainly not their father. The fellow could barely see the fingers in front of his face!

There were expressions of puzzlement and dismay. But the air – the summit-air! The sweet aromas, the Sea-Of-Cairns peering down upon the Great Glinting Ocean?

Their brother waved a dismissive hand.

Summit air – Sweet air – Glinting oceans…' It was all whimsy; the stuff of poets and the feeble-minded. Air was air – and beyond 'indoors' as opposed to 'outdoors', was all much of a muchness.

He extended a hand to meet the troubled looks.

'Think about it!' he said, quick to remind them of the limitation of their options – short of telling the chap his final request was beyond them, and which amongst them would care to go to his grave with *that* on his conscience?

There were furrowed expressions, each accepting privately that maybe their brother had a point, that viable alternatives did appear to be a little thin on the ground. Maybe, just maybe, it would work. There were more exchanged looks and some moments later, a clasping of hands.

'Good lads,' said Jeremiah, all smiles. 'Good lads.'

It would be down to Jeremiah – always destined to be the brains behind the operation – to get things off the ground: preparing them for the task, whilst reminding them of the numerous landmarks and views they'd be obliged to point out en-route. Showing them too how to angle and roll the stretcher in such a way as to give the impression they were mounting a slope as opposed to plodding up and down on the spot. The trick, he insisted, was to make regular stops, at which point they would lay their father to the ground and regale him with the spectacular views and scenes that sadly he was unable to set eyes upon.

Joshua, the eldest, and feeling honour-bound to contribute something of note to proceedings, pointed out the need to convey an impression of actually *ascending* the mountain. Stepping up and down on-the-spot even with a few shakes and tumbles was unlikely to convey the impression they were doing anything beyond suffering an attack of the jitters.

Again Jeremiah had done his homework. The 'leaders' – Joshua and Monserrat 2nd would hoist the stretcher above waist height, whilst behind them – himself and Ezekial would crouch low, holding their ends below waist height – thus holding their father at such an angle as would, indeed, convey the impression they were making their way, albeit slowly, to the summit. At which point the chap would finally be released from their clutches and free to breathe the mountain-air to his heart's content.

And so it came to pass, after some contact with the weathermen, that the following Wednesday, when there would barely be a breath of air to speak of, on or off the mountain, the four gathered at the hospital gates for a quick run-through of the procedure before venturing along the drive to greet their father. The trip from the hospital to the mountain path was some two miles and would be courtesy of the hospital's ambulance, arranged and paid for by their father.

For all the misery of the man's plight, it was a singularly upbeat welcome that greeted them, their father making a show of raising himself on his elbows and permitting himself to be ferried along the lawns to the waiting ambulance. And then later, to be drawn from its rear and carried along the path bordered by grassy tufts to the lower reaches of the valley.

Barely a word was exchanged, as, having reached their predetermined point, the two frontsmen raised the stretcher to just below chest height, the rear bearers lifting it to slightly below waist height.

At a head-nodding count to three, each began a much-rehearsed stepping on-the-spot routine, occasionally tilting the stretcher left and right, adding the odd bobble to account for some misplaced boulder or unforeseen deviation in the path's meandering route.

There would, of course, be banter, and at regular intervals, Jeremiah would draw them to a halt to fill their father in on the increasingly spectacular views stretching out beneath them.

'If only you could see it father,' he would say, waxing lyrical on the quarries and tarns, whilst in reality gazing at little more than a few tufts of grass poking up from the side of the path.

'I see it son. In my mind's eye, I see it as clearly as in my youth – the space, the sky and soon, the Great Glinting Ocean peering up from below.'

The others looked across, a half-scowl serving as a reminder that deceiving their father was one thing, but to goad him thus was perhaps taking things too far. But again, they were a step, if not a dozen steps, behind their brother, whose intent was simply to gauge the extent of their father's senses, or lack of them, rather than seek scorn at his expense.

But, their father appeared to have bought into the mood, urging them to pay heed before setting off once more on the next stage of their trek.

'And – mark you – Only by being here can one appreciate the wholesomeness of it – let no-one tell you otherwise,' he said, wagging a warning finger.

The boys were quick to concur, and equally quick to return to their well-rehearsed routine – stepping up and down on a spot not too visible from the road to town only a few hundred yards to their right.

'Not far now Father,' said Jeremiah some time later, recalling the traverse leading down to the South Ridge, a small seagull conveniently perched on the flange of swampy ground.

'That's right – not so far. Take it all in boys – the aromas of the mountain. For there is no point the length and breadth of the land where the air is so sweet as this.'

'Quite so father – quite so,' confirmed Joshua casting an impish look across the stretcher.

It was after a further half-hour or so's on-the-spot tramping, that – on a final head-count to three – they ceased their steps and lowered the stretcher to the ground, enabling them to take a well-earned rest, their backs drawing little amusement from being required to step up and down on the spot for such a protracted length of time.

'The summit!' announced Jeremiah.

'The summit!' repeated the others, placing their oars to the ground and picking up on Jeremiah's example – bracing themselves with their own deep chunks of mountain air.

'The summit!' breathed their father, but in a softer, more reflective tone. Raising himself and his two eye-pads from the stretcher, he turned an enquiring head this way and that.

'And the Great Ridge. And the Great Glinting Ocean...' He reached out. 'Does it glint boys? Tell me how the ocean glints under the full weight of the afternoon sun.'

'Oh father – it surely glints,' said Montserrat 2nd looking at his watch and the sheepish expressions on the faces opposite.

'Like a forest of tiny diamonds,' added Joshua quickly and arguably picking his words none too cleverly.

'And the air – so rich, so free.' Their father propped himself on his elbows and appeared to remonstrate with the sky.

'Absolutely,' agreed the brothers. 'Absolutely rich and free.'

'Free as a bird,' said Ezekiel, quick to add his own humble contribution from the rear.

It was at that point that their father – ecstatic to an extent they had rarely seen in the man before – laid himself once more upon the stretcher and beckoned the sons to his side.

The sons closed in, anticipating some further observations or maybe a vote of thanks for their efforts and display of loyalty.

But it wasn't quite that.

It was as their father took another bout of bracing summit-air, that proceedings began to take – as they say – a whole new direction.

It was in a quite solemn tone that he begged them listen while he explained that – for reasons that would become apparent – he had been, as they say, a little 'economical with the truth' back in his hospital bed. That there was a detail or two that – for good reason – he had felt necessary to keep from them.

The sons were again all ears, eager hear what latest revelations were to be put their way.

He took them back to a point they themselves had raised at his bedside: the prognosis of the hospital doctor, whose judgements – no doubt blunted by endless eighteen hour stints on the job – had seen fit to be brought into question. For as the boys had rightly pointed out, a chap doesn't lose his sight virtually overnight and for no apparent reason. The fact was that for all his initial posturing, he too had been far from convinced by the explanation on offer.

Which – talking of 'doctors' – made a quite unexpected development shortly after, a singularly fortuitous occasion.

He shifted himself, scratching a finger against a lower lip. As he recalled it was a day or so following the doctor's prognosis that they had been awarded a visit of a travelling apothecary: one of the 'old school', a dying breed in these days of genetic-screening and 3D body-scanners, a chap whose 'art' stems as much from remedies in grandma's kitchen drawer as from the shelves of the hospital library. Yet – a chap prepared to offer hope where it seemed all else had failed. A chap who did the rounds in the hospitals and who – on presenting his calling card – and upon receipt of a few coppers, would undertake his own examination of the case presented before him: in the case of their father, having him rotate the iris and allow a few beads of light through a special lens-glass directly into the film at the rear of the eye-socket.

It was on completion of his examination that a twinkle in the apothecary's eye told its own story; that a rebounding of light had indicated a tiny glint: a case known in medical circles, as 'sleeping eye': a rare though not unknown phenomena in the case of those born and reared in the shadow of The Mountain. And – unbeknown to many – quite curable, requiring little more than a moment's exposure to the air at The Mountain Summit. The rest, maybe, they could guess for themselves.

To the sons it was all getting a little too much. 'Summit air', 'travelling quacks.' At that moment bolts of lightning from the heavens would have come as no great surprise.

And might have been a preferred option to watching their father reach behind his head to begin a ceremonial unveiling of both eyes!

First to react was Jeremiah, stepping across, if only to buy a little time. He quickly halted his father in his tracks.

'Whoa father – slow – slow. For mightn't removing the bandages in one fell swoop be a little drastic after being denied light for so long?'

The others, catching on, leapt to offer support. 'Surely father, that *was* a point.'

Their father thought a moment. Perhaps he was right. Why risk sacrificing the ship for a ha'pworth of tar? The pause was sufficient to have the lads form another huddle some distance from the stretcher.

Another conundrum that they hadn't bargained for.

'Stuff and nonsense,' said Ezekial, picking up his brother's line from a few days back.

'Eyesight back – Summit-air...Witchdoctor waffle.'

He looked across to the man, his pale features hidden by two thick white pads, still clinging blindly to the valley sky.

'Hmm. Maybe – maybe not,' said Jeremiah, eyeing the stretcher, his voice wavering just a fraction.

Each knew they had – albeit unwittingly – bitten off rather more than they had bargained for. The facts were simple enough: 'witchdoctor waffle' or not, their father had been offered a last-ditch chance to maybe see the light of day once more, the ins and outs of which – for the time being at least – were neither here nor there. Were they to stand in his path?

'But – we're nowhere near the summit,' pointed out Ezekiel, eyeing the lines of cars toe-to-tail along the road to town some two to three hundred yards to his right.

'Tush...Summit air! – Glinting oceans – it's all hogwash anyway,' pointed out Joshua, seeking to return them to their original premise.

'But – if he believes it!'

There was a shrugging of shoulders.

'So what if he believes it – we're four thousand feet beneath it!'

There were more searching looks and an earnest scratching of heads. They needed to act quickly. To dilly and dally would simply add fuel to the notion something could be afoot and perhaps prompt the chap to take his chance with the summit-air as prescribed.

'So – father.' Jeremiah was first back on the scene, kneeling aside the stretcher.

'We've been thinking – to take the pads away at such short notice could be risky. For the likelihood is...such magic as your apothecary speaks of is___'

He thought a moment, scratching his chin as was his habit when seeking moments of inspiration. 'Likely a slow-burning process, one that takes its time to infiltrate itself into the nerves of the brain.' There were nods from all sides. His brothers had heard as much.

'So...' said Joshua, kneeling close enough to pick up the reins from there.

'Faith father! Surely that is the name of the game.' He leant, gripping his father's hand more tightly.

'What say we get you off the mountain first, give the summit air chance to perform its tricks. And then maybe have you back on the road to recovery.'

The father was silent a moment, his eye-pads turning in roughly the direction of the four sons in turn.

'You think so?'

'Undoubtedly father – undoubtedly,' said Jeremiah quick to take advantage of a moment's hesitation.

'Hmm.' Their father laid back, chomping and grinding his jaw, a habit of his when required to mull things over for any length of time.

'But surely, a taste of the air – just a smidgeon under the pads could help.'

The boys exchanged looks. A conciliatory tactic maybe. And where was the harm? The chap could barely see the fingers on the end of his hands.

'Okay father, but a mere smidgeon…' Joshua advised, steadying his father's chin and raising each pad a few centimetres from the eye for a few seconds, lest anything of their surroundings be captured in an involuntary blink. Then quickly replacing the pads and slapping the man gently on the shoulder.

'Okay,' he announced, reaching for the stretcher's flank as invitation for the others to follow suit and hit the slope once more, this time, in a thankfully more agreeable descending direction.

The sons wiped a few kilos of sweat from their brows and made quick grabs for their corners lest the chap should suffer a second 'visitation' and a change of heart; the secret of the mountain's summit-air – at least for the moment – seeming destined to remain on-ice.

What *was* clear was that the descent would be a more rapid business than the ascent –the increase in pace allowing them to trot a little quicker, giving the stretcher a few extra shakes for their trouble. Plus – the amazing views across the valley finally being dispensed with.

'Not far now,' said Ezekiel, giving the stretcher an extra tumble or two in simulation of their more rapid progress.

'No not long,' sighed their father. 'Until I shall see the birds, the flowers, the sky and, of course, my four fine sons,' he added, not wishing to be seen as too unproprietal in his ambitions.

'Maybe father, maybe,' said Joshua, staring blankly at the faces opposite.

'We'll see father, we'll see,' added Jeremiah, similarly keen to temper any untoward strains of optimism and only later questioning the appropriateness of his words.

Their father laughed.

'Faith lads! Have a little faith…These apothecary chaps go back to a time before X-ray machines and stethoscopes were even dreamt of. Tradition! Not to be scorned, always remember that!' He waved a finger and gripped the sides of the stretcher in time to negotiate a particularly rocky stretch of the path's descent.

It was some half hour later, with the events of the day rapidly drifting beyond any of their control, that – with some apprehension – they lowered the stretcher to the ground upon which they had been plodding for the last several hours and more.

Seeing any man – particularly their father – pin such hopes on the vagaries of some wandering apothecary was a sorry sight. Yet – to have denied the man his one lingering hope of seeing the world and those who dwell upon it once more was an equally painful cross to bear. It seemed, in many ways, they were back to the conundrum of the hospital room!

But what's done was done, and if this was the price to be paid for their part in the charade, who were they to complain?

Reduced to roles of abject bystanders, they watched as their father reached behind his head and – with a magician's flick of the wrist – whipped the two ends of the bandages apart to lift the pads from the whites of his eyes.

To his right – the green grass of the field. Above – the clear blue of the sky. And to his left – the awe-struck faces of his four sons.

The man's face broke as if eyeing the chaps for the first time since their moment of birth – both arms raised to the air in a gesture of triumph.

'I see...I see,' the claim rang out along half the length of the valley.

His sons stared – at the sky – at the green field that surrounded them – at their father and finally, at each other.

'Father!'

'I see sons. I see!' repeated their father with a thrust of the right fist and barely daring to believe what any of them would have thought even remotely possible.

He sighed and extended an arm and eyes – each in exceptional working order – in the direction of his sons.

'See chaps...A little belief!'

'Quite so,' concurred the sons, the day and all that had passed before it suddenly beginning to swim before their eyes.

Their father allowed a moment's reprieve before drawing the bandages into a ball and placing them behind him on the stretcher.

Reaching an arm across the nearest shoulders, he proceeded to rise from the stretcher, flexing first one leg and then the other in an attempt to shake off a few months inactivity, and began striding effortlessly across the tufts of grass.

A few yards on he stopped and turned, a look of triumph meeting the line of dumbfounded faces, only Jeremiah finding it in himself to recover his power of speech.

'Father – you're walking. You have found your legs!'

Their father chuckled and bowed a head in confirmation of the fact.

'True son – true,' he said.

'But – How?'

An arm was raised to meet their troubled looks.

'Relax,' he said, continuing to eye the glazed expressions with some amusement.

He took a few more steps, returning to his stretcher and reaching to lift the mattress, folded it and tucked it tightly under one arm.

Seconds later, the five were trotting in a line back across the field, their father leading the way, drawing them to a halt by the gate. He stopped to look back, eyeing the slopes of the mountain reaching to the dizzy heights of The Summit.

'It was the apothecary's deal. A special offer – two for the price of one!'

He stopped again, giving each leg a thorough shake to remove blades of grass from the cuffs of his hospital strides.

'How could I resist? And – let's face it – what did I have to lose?'

He flexed the knee joint, watching the cuff drop back into place on the right boot.

'And...I had to have some means of getting up there – you understand that don't you?

He drew an arm across their aching shoulders, urging them to join him in a moment's reflection.

'Put yourself in my place. What sort of father puts his sons under an obligation to perform miracles – and at the whim of some travelling-quack? Think boys…think.'

He stopped to give each a resounding thump on the shoulder.

'And, I take my hat off to you. It was a stirring day's work. For many a son would have said 'stuff that' the moment such a proposition was even raised.'

He stopped again, a twinkle evident in each fully-functioning eye.

'A little belief eh lads…a little faith?…And…an excellent idea not to dilly dally at the summit.' He smacked the base of his strides a little more vigorously and turned his attention to the gate stood in their path a few feet away.

Somewhat exhausted by the events of the day, the sons began to plod their way to the road. Only Jeremiah stood back – watching as his father hesitated before taking the gate in a single leap and bringing them to order with a sudden clap of hands.

'Now – unless I'm much mistaken The Red Lion has been open some half an hour. What say we stop off for a few on the way back? And these are on me. For it was not an easy conundrum to be faced with – and you tackled it with some aplomb. Good lads…good lads!'

The sons exchanged looks but said nothing.

Jeremiah – one step ahead of the others – was looking back over his shoulder, thinking a visit to the mountain's summit might not be a bad idea, not only to take in the air, which – aside from its renown medicinal qualities – was also an ideal spot to get a bit of peace and quiet!

The Queen's Speech

To Her Majesty it wasn't so much the *heat* – or the food – as the hangers-on: the ragbag of sycophants and their tiresome tickle-tackle that were a pain in the butt; that – and their inability to breathe a word without endlessly referring to their wretched phrasebooks!

Two hours into the new day – a cloudless sky already spreading into the far reaches of the firmament, the wagon barely breaching the Palace walls, and already they were at it – the phrase-books flapping, the banalities raining in on her from all sides....

And how was Her Majesty this morning? How was her 'nice cup of tea? Hopefully not too strong. Hopefully not too weak. And the weather? Hopefully not too hot. Hopefully not too cold. Somewhere in between perhaps, as if it can't quite make up its mind...

There were sniggers from the back row and blank looks from the Chiefs-Of-Staff whose understanding of such things – or anything come to that – was virtually zilch!

It was as the carriage turned into yet another street packed with flag-wavers and hysterical cheering, that Her Majesty – seeking temporary escape and a moment's quiet reflection in the scene beyond the carriage window – uttered a few well-chosen words....

A rapid exchange of looks was followed by a frantic toing and froing of the phrase-book's pages.

Her Majesty had spoken – but what had she said?

Why does she insist on levelling what few words she ever utters to those lining the streets beyond the carriage window? Looks were extended in their direction.

'Something about the *poor* people,' one surmised, craning her neck in the direction of the crowds gesticulating wildly from the sidelines.

'That's what it sounded like to me,' said another, following her gaze.

'Giving her a headache,' agreed a third, perched somewhere at the rear.

'*Poor* people giving Her Majesty a headache...' 'Well, really...'

Heads turned in all directions.

The Emperor's secretary, quickly on hand, stabbed a finger at the pane of glass.

'These wretched oafs,' he said, indicating the hordes whooping and hollering as if from the deck of a drowning ship. 'Clogging the streets with their tiresome flags, giving Her Majesty the most monumental of headaches. Just who do they think they are?"

'The sun doesn't help...' put in one sitting near the back.

'There's a lot of it about,' added another, nodding in agreement.

'Tell me about it...' said a third.

'It's a no-brainer...'

There were more sniggers on the back row.

And – consternation from all sides.

The Chiefs-Of-Staff exchanged looks. A grim-faced secretary reached for the phone to relay Her Majesty's message to the Emperor's Palace....That the *poor* people – the 'Unmentionables' lining the streets mile after mile – *were giving Her Majesty an infernal headache!*

Back at the Palace the accusations flew. Questions passed down the line as to just who had given permission for the streets to be cluttered in such a fashion, flagging Her Majesty down every inch of the route. It was enough to give anyone a headache!

Minutes later the phone rang – an edict had been dispatched.

It was with some relief that the secretary replaced the phone and turned to the Chiefs-Of-Staff who, in turn, turned to the lines of lackeys with a warning to be a little more mindful of Her Majesty's tongue from here-on.

It was the following day, as the sun arched a familiar route over the corrugated rooftops some distance from the palace grounds, that the first of the bulldozers moved in, reducing its shacks to rubble and tumbling them into skips to be shifted at some later date to some predetermined spot in the middle of the desert. Shack after shack, mile after mile. Nothing would be left to chance: domiciles to some of the planet's most impoverished, down-trodden folk tumbled into jumbo-sized skips to be whipped away at Her Majesty's convenience – and from the eye of those whose sad lot had been to witness the scene through windows en-route to their offices in the mornings.

Back at the Palace there was much clashing of champagne glasses and a satisfied brushing of hands. They'd done well there – eradicating the root of Her Majesty's displeasure...And finally getting round to kick-starting phase-one of the nation's housing programme – all, as the phrasebooks have it, in 'one-fell-swoop'!

'All's well that ends well,' came the communal cry, midst much guffawing and mutual slapping of backs.

And so it was with a spring in their step and an uplift in spirit that the entourage settled into their places for the following day's round-the-houses tour from the Palace grounds.

Yet, as far as Her Majesty was concerned, little, it seemed, had changed.

No sooner had they breached the Palace gates than the pack was back: the banalities raining in on her from seemingly every angle.....

And how was Her Majesty this morning? She was looking a bit pale. A bit knackered...? Well we're all a bit knackered. It's the weather. There's something going round....

Once again, Her Majesty found herself gazing disconsolately through the carriage window. Yet even the streets brought scant relief – the cheering throngs of the previous tour having – for some reason – been replaced by heaps of corrugated tin dumped into giant skips – a few limbs poking out here and there, as if in some parting salutary gesture.

The entourage was at a loss. Was Her Majesty ill? Bit of a headache still? Bit knackered? It's the sun. There's a lot of it about. There's something going round. Could be the weather – one day this, one day *that* – never seeming able to make up its mind...!

There were more sniggers on the back row.

Finally Her Majesty could take no more. She turned, this time making a point of addressing the Emperor's Secretary himself – full on!

'Look,' she said, her frustration evident in each clearly enunciated syllable...

'I said it yesterday and I'll say it again... *Your* people *really do* give me a headache!'

The Emperor's Secretary – temporarily lost for words – raised the receiver of his phone. And then, thinking better of it – replaced it.

[Based on an old African folk tale]

The Hitchhiker's Tale

A truck driver emerged from the subdued light of the cafe, wiped a hand across his jaw and made his way to where his truck had been waiting patiently some forty, forty-five minutes on one of the bays at the far end of the lot. A full belly and several strong coffees had livened his step and steeled his resolve to make it to his appointed spot by sundown – likely some six hours hence.

He was at the point of reaching for the handle when a voice broke from somewhere round the rear: a high pitched voice – sharp and clear in the relative calm of the afternoon.

'Okay mister.'

He turned, ever-wary of voices springing out of nowhere – particularly from the rear of his parked truck.

Leaning against its corner was a youngish man: mid-late thirties, lean-built, dressed casual in working Levis, open necked collar shirt and lightweight hunter's jacket, topped, in true showman-style, by a wide-brimmed kaki cowboy hat which – cast against the rear of a transport truck and above a thin weasely face – looked either cute or plain silly, depending on which way you looked at it. Having offered his greeting he drew alongside the truck – his movements easy and relaxed. He doffed the hat and nodded at the door that the driver was about to reach for.

'Chance of a lift?' he asked, his voice bright and breezy, the hat raised a fraction.

'Heading Lewisville way and sure could use a little help – if you'd be obliged,' he added, looking round. The driver flicked his own hat and turned his eye on the road ahead.

'Where you from?' he asked, searching beyond the man's dead-pan expression.

'Round Telluside, Mesa-Verda region, but I gotta head on north; try to get to Lewisville, then across to Oklahoma City, though I ain't too sure 'bout when that's gonna be.'

The man looked east, mapping his route in his mind before turning again to the driver, a foot levelled ready on the footplate.

The driver was figuring it would be a hundred, maybe hundred twenty miles or so to his next planned break, possibly a truckstop somewhere along the line – perhaps a little company wouldn't hurt for a while.

He gave the rider – and his hat – a final once-over and nodded towards the far side of the cab.

'Okay, guess I can manage couple o' hours further.'

The man nodded and doffed his hat once more.

'Thanks, much 'ppreciate it.'

Doors opened and clanked shut and within seconds, the flat tarmac of the lot was behind them, the open road beckoning.

The driver gave his window handle a couple of turns for a breeze to clear the confined space of the cab. His rider, slipping a shoulder bag onto his lap, had his eye fixed on the road ahead.

'What they call ya?' he asked, interrupting his view to eye the driver more closely.

'Billy,' said the driver, bracing himself for the obligatory exchanges.

'Eddie.' The rider extended a hand which, out of courtesy, was briefly accepted. Billy returned to the wheel and a packet of tobacco taken from his pocket.

'Come far?' Eddie watched as Billy settled his forearms against the upper rim of the wheel, the tobacco near enough rolling itself between the thin lines of paper. The cigarette needed igniting before an answer could follow. And a few inhalations. 'Arizona.'

Eddie too reached for his jacket, drawing a packet of Marlboros from a side pocket.

He nodded at the driver, popping the cigarette between his lips and lighting it instantly.

'Wish I had your patience.' He cocked an eye at the tobacco pouch returned to within grabbing distance on the dashboard and exhaled through the open window.

The road was a straight-as-a-dye, roller-coaster stretch starting from the fringes of the south-east plains, taking them up towards the valleys of the north; oil-painting country through most of the summertime, with the likelihood of a good empty ride as far as the shadows of the upper slopes, hopefully by nightfall.

Eddie blew smoke and drifted his attentions to back within the cab.

'You allowed to take on riders or don't it really matter when you get out these parts?' he said.

Billy shrugged. Fact was he neither knew, nor particularly cared. Eddie eased himself back and hooked his hat a little lower.

'S'pose it gives a guy chance to think, drivin' the highways day after day.'

As if in demonstration of the point, he eased himself back in the seat.

'Yer married?'

Billy checked the mirror and thought about it a moment.

'Yeah...' he said, finally prepared to concede the fact. 'I'm married.'

Eddie checked the mirror and peered casually at the Holiday Inn's affirmation *'The best surprise is no surprise at all'* rapidly passing him by on the right hand side.

'Yer from Houston?'

Billy was taking note of the mileage – a mental note of his workload since the crack of dawn.

'Nah, from Missouri originally – Grand Forks – Red River Valley,' he said. 'Been livin' in Houston last five years.'

Eddie raised an eye.

'Houston huh? One crazy beast of a city – I know Houston pretty good – suffocatin' kind of a place ain't it?'

Billy shrugged.

Eddie closed his eyes, settled his feet against the dash and nudged the hat. He raised an eye before he spoke.

'Was married myself a while back,' he said, manoeuvring the hat a little more to keep the sun from his face.

He drew on his cigarette and stared through the open window. 'Nice looking gal. Bouncing hair and big blue eyes…I like a gal with big blue eyes,' he said with a laugh, his eye strutting to and fro across Billy's deadpan expression.

'Good shoulders too – neat and round.' He paused to lean forward, tapping the ash gently into the tray on the dash.

'Trouble was….She was just a little *too* pretty, if you know what I mean? Them blue eyes just a little *too* big, seein' a little more than was good for 'em, if you get my drift.'

He flicked the hat and settled back in his seat.

'Got to be looking round all over the goddamn place,' he said. 'Particularly two doors along from where we was livin'.'

Beneath the cowboy hat, the eyes narrowed, picturing a now all-too-familiar scene: a young couple strutting hand-in-hand by a lumber-fronted block with its neat lines of steps and shuttered windows – idyllic setting for a couple setting out on their own little adventure together.

'Took a while to get the place,' he said. 'Finally got it from a guy got a string of stores and a couple of downtown bars. Decent looking place.' He drew meditatively on the cigarette. 'Guy few doors down was a Puerto-Rican fella – twenty two – big guy – good-looking – single.' He tipped the ash in the tray and leant back.

'We had a good thing goin' No need for her to go doin' what she done.'

He closed his eyes and drew the hat lower. 'Balling the guy. She ruined everything.'

His eyes narrowed and he looked quickly to his left.

'So I whacked her.'

He levelled a finger just behind his ear. '*Two* bullets.' He dipped his hat and looked across the dash.

'I ain't got no problem whackin' a woman who done what she done. Anyone doin' what she done's asking to get whacked. That's why I whacked her... *Two* bullets.'

He twisted the cigarette stub to a ball in the tray and slumped in the seat, turning to Billy as if expecting to see some reaction. Billy reached into his pocket for a packet of gum.

Eddie focused his eye on the dashes of tarmac rapidly disappearing under the truck's wheels. He waited – picking his moment.

'But then, that ain't the end of it. She's lying there, whacked, thinking...it's an end to it. Well fact is it ain't – *she* fucks things up – sure, but so does *he*.'

He stared out – his attention seized by a bank of trees and criss-cross fencing forming a border to a passing homestead – by its side, a youngish couple, strolling hand-in-hand alongside a long white fence running down to a tumbling stream.

'So I pay our sweet-talking Puerto-Rican friend a little visit. Big guy – you know what I mean? Big fella. Good-looking guy too, so they say. So I brought him down to earth a little – rearranged his looks...whacked him – two bullets.'

He drew a finger level with his temple and quickly looked away.

For some moments the purr of the engine was interrupted only by a packet levelled across the cab from Billy's right hand. Eddie reached across to withdraw a strip of gum.

'Guess you're wondrin' why I'm tellin' you all this,' he said. 'Don't suppose it's every day a guy gets in yer truck and gives the low-down on how he whacked his missus.'

Billy shrugged. It was no business of his. He had a wife of his own waiting at home.

Eddie removed the film and screwed it to a tiny ball, reaching across to deposit it in the tray of the dash.

'Or maybe you're just figuring I'm nuts,' he added, looking up and grinning.

The only thing Billy was figuring was to keep his eye on the road. He'd met guys like Eddie before – guys who spent their lives searching for someone's ear to bend – some shoulder to lean on – cry on too when it all started to get a little too much.

Eddie chewed, waiting to pick his moment.

'Trouble is,' he said. 'The guy in the apartment upstairs – I happen to know was *not* the first...'

He settled back, raising his hat a fraction so as not to interrupt his view.

'Seems that before him, there was another guy – a guy she'd been seeing about six months, in a motel.' He lit another Marlboro, exhaling noisily and tapping the bag sitting in his lap.

'Motel they'd been renting out near the freeway – Gulf freeway, dunno if you know the neighborhood.' He looked across.

Whether he did or he didn't appeared to get little more than a passing thought. Billy was taking repeated glances at his watch. He'd been thinking in terms of a stop in another ten miles or so. It seemed like a good idea – get a little air, stretch the feet, get Eddie walking around a little, take his mind off things. Maybe do the pair of them a bit of good.

It was shortly after that Eddie looked across to see Billy apparently distracted by something to the right. He leant forwards to look more closely to the front side of the hood.

Eddie, silent a moment, was watching him.

'Problem?' he asked.

Billy stalled a little on the gas to listen more closely. He shrugged and looked across at Eddie.

'Could be,' he said. 'You hear anything?'

Eddie shrugged. Engines were as much a mystery to him as to the Chief of the Blackfoot Indians.

'Hear a revvin' sound,' he said vaguely.

Billy lent forwards a little more, his foot held in a steady position, taking care not to put too much pressure on the feed of gas.

'Yeh, that's what I'm hearin'. Means something ain't right. Gonna take a stop,' he announced.

Eddie looked out across the wide open spaces, the only sign of life – a few scurries of cloud drifting over the lower reaches of the distant hills.

Having checked in the mirror, Billy eased pressure on the pedal and drew the truck to a standstill on the right shoulder. He turned the key and looked towards the front side of the hood.

'I could use a little help,' he said.

Eddie looked vaguely at the area that seemed to be causing concern.

'What?' he asked.

Billy nodded through the windscreen.

'I need you to tell me if you see anything dripping from a tube running just underneath the engine. Difficult to do it myself. I gotta step on the gas see if it's leaking any.'

Eddie thought for a minute. He was no mechanic. He guessed it made sense to check out these things sooner rather than later.

'Okay,' he said.

Billy allowed him time to turn for the door and reach for the handle.

'Just stand over the engine,' he said, watching as Eddie reached for the lever and stepped outside.

'I'll release the hood,' said Billy. 'And tell you what to do.'

The moment Eddie's foot touched the ground was the moment Billy hit the gas.

Eddie had vague recollections of spinning into the roadside and lying alongside it for a moment, a blazing soreness from his hip finally registering on his brain. Heaving himself into a sitting position, he reached down, spreading a wetness across his lower shirt. He looked down. His hand was coated in blood. For a moment he wondered if he'd been shot.

His eye turned to the truck, watching as Billy eased it back onto the main artery of the road. Staggering to his feet, he brushed himself down and reached for the bag dumped against the verge. There was little to be gained from looking at his watch.

He surveyed the scene, squinting his eye against the sun sinking rapidly over the grey blue line of mountains. This place was out of it; a guy could die around here. Should've whacked the guy back in the lot.

He glanced left and right and – hat pulled low, hands thrust in pockets – started walking.

Mr. Atkinson's Funeral

A man, advanced by some years beyond his forties' style grey trilby and long-frocked coat, cast an eye over the awning at the building's entrance and perused the plaques displayed at its side. It was certainly the place – the few facts he could glean from the wall echoing the details he'd gathered beforehand.

A glass swing-door revolved him into a pinewood decked foyer – a spacious arrangement, lined with a few easy-on-the-eye paintings and equally easy-on-the-eye chairs. A desk stretched the length of the right hand side. And behind it – a woman, in 'company policy' plain grey skirt, open necked lemon blouse, and a tiny bud pinned onto her lapel. She looked up from her computer screen and offered a welcoming smile as he drew close enough to lean against the pinewood panelling.

'Can I help you sir?' she asked.

Her visitor looked round – a quick overview of the place and then of the face he was about to address. She was perhaps mid-twenties, quite attractive in a clipped contrived sort of way.

'Hopefully,' he said, pausing only to pop his hat on the desk and clear his throat. He leant closer, looking the woman firmly in the eye.

'I'd like to book a funeral,' he said.

'Right sir. One moment please.'

The woman reached routinely for a small book sitting on her right hand side.

'Okay, I need to take some details.' She took the pen and placed a carbon sheet and resting card under the top copy.

Her manner, like her looks, was bright and unruffled: indication of a clear uncluttered approach as befits one employed in such a business as theirs.

She coughed lightly, reaching for her pen.

'Right sir, could I have the name of the deceased please?'

She waited, poised to push on with what she had every right to assume would be a straightforward booking, giving her chance to get on with the floral decorations for a *Celebration Of A Life* later that afternoon. The man waited too. He wanted to be sure she got the details correct.

'Yes – it's me,' he said, leaning casually against the desk and looking the woman firmly in the eye.

'Sorry....' She laid her pad to one side, assuming he must, for some reason, have misheard her.

'It's my funeral,' he explained.

'I'm sorry sir, I don't quite understand. This is 'The Pathe/Lane Funeral Commemoration Service.'

'Yes I know. And I want to book one.' He leant more firmly against the counter, eyeing a calendar and tiny vase of plastic flowers.

'For yourself,' she said, wary of needing to have the point clarified.

'Correct.' He placed his folded arms on the counter and glanced left and right.

She awarded him one of her more diplomatic smiles – an effective ploy from time to time in the case of one or two of the punters. He seemed sane enough – a little greyed at the edges, but actually quite dignified-looking in his *Fifties – Hollywood*-style coat and matching trilby.

'Sir... you're still alive?' she said.

He stared hard at the desk and looked up.

'I know,' he said, tapping his fingers in confirmation of the fact. 'I said I wish to book a funeral. I didn't say anything about dying.'

She replaced her pen, urging him to bear with her a moment as she turned to pick up the phone. He nodded and looked away, his fingers still tapping patiently on the desk.

A minute later, the doors opened at the far end of the foyer and a figure emerged to make his way towards them. He was perhaps early-thirties – neat and dapper in company-policy plain grey suit, plain tie and white collared shirt. He too extended a welcoming smile and accompanying hand to the man standing at the desk.

'Darmi Pathe,' he announced in a bright breezy manner – one no doubt accustomed to sorting these minor misunderstandings at the drop of a hat. He extended an arm, leading the man to one side.

'Okay sir, now, if you could just run the details by me one more time just to check that we're getting it clear.'

He made a point of avoiding the eye of his secretary who had already made a hasty retreat to her computer screen.

'I wish to book a funeral,' the man repeated, hopeful of being able to get down to a few details without too long a delay.

'Well that's what we're here for,' said Darmi, still smiling.

'And just to clarify – *Whose* funeral is this?'

'Mine.'

'Okay, fine.'

Darmi rose to his feet and gestured towards a door at the rear of the foyer.

Moments later, each had taken their seat either side of a large pinewood desk. Darmi leant forward – seeking to follow his secretary's example in buying a little time.

'Mr Atkinson, let me just check I've got this right. You wish to book a funeral – your own funeral.'

'That's correct.'

Darmi tapped his pen.

'Even though you're not dead,' he said, speaking in the tone of one accustomed to dealing with the more unconventional demands of the business.

'Correct,' said Mr. Atkinson, speaking, for his part, with exaggerated patience, as if still in the process of confirming a few details back at the desk.

Darmi leant across the desk making every effort *not* to look his client too firmly in the eye.

'Sir, I have to ask – are you ill?'

Mr. Atkinson shifted in his seat and looked up.

'No more than one would expect from a man in my position,' he said, looking fleetingly along extended arms and speaking as one might when quoting word for word from one's own medical report. Darmi tapped his fingers. There was another possibility that couldn't easily be avoided. He struggled at first, looking self-consciously at the desk.

'Mr. Atkinson. Forgive me asking this. But I hope you'll understand *my* position.'

He coughed again, feeling obliged, just this once, to look the man firmly in the eye. 'Does an intention to take your own life lie anywhere in your plans?'

Mr. Atkinson eyed him equally squarely, and then appeared to relent. He eased himself back in his seat.

'You needn't worry on that score…But I understand you asking,' he said, coughing lightly and switching his attention to his hat.

Darmi's eyes narrowed as he began to shuffle a handful of papers stacked in his desk.

Sensing a need to seize the initiative a little, Mr. Atkinson eased himself forward.

'Let me explain,' he said. 'It's really quite simple.' He had his hands drawn across the top of the desk. He thought for a moment.

'There have been – thus far – two main events in my life…my *birth* which, by all accounts, I was present at…my *marriage* which I was present at; the third…my *funeral*..is' He hesitated, allowing time for the appropriate phrase to spring to mind. 'Reasonably imminent, if not immediately so. And I would like to be around for that too…'

At which he eased back into his seat, resuming a slow rotation of the hat though his fingers.

'You see – if I was dead I'd miss out on proceedings. I wouldn't be around to feel part of it and hear what was said. Which seems a shame really. I'd rather like to witness the event for myself.'

Darmi continued to eye the figure seated opposite. There was an air of resignation, a calmness almost about the man that was as unnerving as it was reassuring, prompting him to lend a closer ear. Maybe the man had a point; Darmi was, after all, no priest; he was a business-man, co-owner of a firm whose business was to arrange and oversee these events – not stand on ceremony as to who should, or shouldn't, be in attendance at them.

The pen tapped more urgently. Time for a little relief in the *Company Tour* – an integral feature of all preliminary negotiations.

The pair made their way to a door at the far end and rang a small bell. A warden opened the door – a young to middle-aged woman dressed in company-policy grey skirt and matching cardigan and open collar. A small bud was pinned to her lapel. At the sight of a client she smiled and turned a respectful eye to her superior.

'Hilary – give me the screen, the lights on rear and front.'

'Yes sir.' His eyes followed her as she made an about turn to attend to a series of switches behind a small door set in the wall. Darmi turned to his client.

'Hilary's our Chief-Warden; oversees the nuts-and-bolts, makes sure the pieces are in place and ready to fit together, like clockwork – on the dot – no fuss, no questions asked. A remarkable woman,' he said, continuing to observe her at some length whilst quickly straightening his tie, giving his flanks and lapel a quick brush-down and leading the way to a large door at the end of the corridor, above which, the words...

In Life And In Love We Share

were embossed in a wreath of italic gold-leaf font. Darmi extended an arm.

'The 'celebration of a life' Mr. Atkinson, that's what we're about. Acknowledging the dignity and privilege of that most precious of gifts.'

Mr. Atkinson nodded and glanced at his watch. Darmi was already looking to the end of the main corridor. He waited to usher his client through a bold pinewood door, opening it and standing aside.

It had the appearance and intimacy of a compact theatre, the forum (auditorium) comprising several rows of seats extending from stage to rear. The stage was equally compact, comprising two lecterns for simultaneous presentations, one at each end, and backed by a curtain stretching the full width.

But it was the rear of the forum that had immediately caught Mr. Atkinson's eye: a small cabin-like affair, rather like a light-house lookout, with what appeared to be a small port-hole window; the possibility already looming large in his mind. He nodded – directing Darmi's eye towards the object of his attention. 'Ah…The Cabin,' said Darmi.

He was already pacing his way towards the steps to the rear.

Once there, he took a key and opened a door on the right hand side.

Fittingly enough, simplicity was its overriding feature. Its main purpose: to provide the facility for the event/commemoration/celebration to be recorded…via audio and/or on film or digitally. Mr. Atkinson was quick to place himself in front of the port-hole, peering into the pit of the auditorium nodding approvingly – withdrawing with a nod at Darmi, standing close by.

'Good view,' he said, looking back at what, from such a close angle, was a tiny aperture sitting in the cabin wall.

'Absolutely,' said Darmi. 'Very good view.'

A stool was placed beneath the aperture and two speakers were built into the sides, allowing the sound to be transmitted clearly into the cabin's interior.

Mr. Atkinson looked round and shifted away, lifting his hat from the stool, a final glance sufficient to confirm The Cabin's capabilities.

He turned to Darmi, shuffling the hat from one hand to the other – privately speculating as to whether getting down to a few details was likely to appear on the agenda or whether his request had already been given the thumbs down.

'So....Mr. Pathe...' he said, shuffling the hat and looking up.

Darmi thought a moment.

'Follow me,' he said.

Having led his client back through the door he turned and began the descent to the main body of the theatre. He was still looking urgently at his watch. *A Celebration Of A Life* was due in approximately two hours time.

Back in the office, Mr. Atkinson took his seat, drawing the folds of his coat across the bridge of his knees. Darmi – making every effort to regard Mr. Atkinson's proposal as he would any other – eased across the desk, tapping the pen routinely against the pinewood top.

There would always be times when the nut-and-bolts of the business struggled to sit comfortably alongside such ethereal issues as 'life' and 'death', but rarely had they encountered such blurred defining lines as this. There was no denying a certain logic in the man's thinking, if *logic* was the right word. And Darmi was, as he was often at pains to remind himself, no priest; he was a 'co-ordinator of services' – a humble small-time operator whose terms-of-reference, as far as he knew, had little to say about a man's right to be present at his own funeral.

He frowned, tapping the pen a little harder.

'Mr. Atkinson...there's something I'm not too clear on,' he said, seeking a return to more practical matters. 'Your – er – congregation...guests. Do you intend them to be a party to your arrangement?' An obvious enough question. Mr. Atkinson looked up.

'No,' he said. 'It wouldn't work that way. To all intents and purposes I will have parted company. Otherwise it wouldn't be fair.'

Choosing to overlook the closing observation, Darmi raised an eye – intrigued, if a little wary as to enquiring exactly *how* the arrangement, if 'arrangement' was the right word, would work out in practice.

'Mr. Atkinson, that being the case, how exactly do you envisage arranging your – shall we say – demise, if you don't mind me asking?'

Mr. Atkinson continued to pass the hat playfully through his fingers, as if running the idea through his mind one final time. He edged closer.

'I will disappear – like Sherlock Holmes at the Reichenbach Falls – in Switzerland. End my days with a little bee-keeping amongst the Swiss alps.' he said. 'It's all sorted. I have connections out there – based in Basle.'

He continued to look down, fumbling for a moment.

Darmi stopped tapping the pen – a few pieces perhaps beginning to slot a little more firmly into place. He looked up, ever-wary of being seen to extend his brief, yet aware too that there were occasionally issues that gained little from being ignored.

'Mr. Atkinson,' he said, struggling, for once, to speak in anything above the gravest of voices.

'Forgive me asking but – isn't all this a bit hard on your wife?'

Mr. Atkinson thought for a moment, perhaps struggling himself to find the appropriate voice.

'Maybe,' he began. He looked up, meeting Darmi's eye full on. 'But would it be kinder to lie – emaciated and bed-ridden – hooked to oxygen cylinders and beeping, flashing monitor screens – my wife sitting at my side, powerless to intervene?'

Darmi's eye caught the bowed figure, fingers clenched tightly in his lap. Moments later, he extended a hand.

'A Celebration Of A Life' Mr. Atkinson,' he said. 'That's what we're about here – nothing more, nothing less.'

Mr. Atkinson looked up.

'Thankyou Mr. Pathe,' he said.

It was some thirty minutes later, that Darmi and his secretary stood in the awning of the entrance foyer, acknowledging

Mr. Atkinson's departure with a shake of the hand. A date and time had been fixed, the arrangements already in hand.

Weather-wise, the gods had been with them and would continue so for the remainder of the day; a slight breeze was blowing, but it seemed to bring a warmth rather than any chill to proceedings.

Ahead of them, pacing himself alongside the sloping lawns and immaculately kept gardens, Mr. Atkinson pulled the collar tight against his neck and drew the trilby firmly on his head.

It was as he approached the gate that Darmi turned to his secretary.

'I think we're looking at a sick man,' he said, his eye following the figure through the wrought-iron gate.

His secretary had been watching him too.

'Mm – I was thinking that,' she said.

Maximus – Plus

The place – *High-Jinks* as it was brazenly advertised in an attempt to catch the more discerning eye from each and every corner of the street – was beginning to get into its stride. At one end, a few lads, bottles in hand. At the other, a smattering of couples standing or seated at tables, a little light conversation, bottle of wine, muted speculation as to how events seemed likely to unfold. Whilst roughly equidistant from any of them, seated on a stool at the bar, Maximus-Plus appeared to be marking time – observing the jagged colours on the wall opposite and the equally garish-looking drinks periodically passed over the bar by a young man pacing back and forth in a black and white tuxedo-style jacket. At regular intervals his own bottle was raised to mouth, dispensing a fraction of its contents into his stomach-lining.

It was at approximately the fourteenth raising of the bottle that the door at the far end opened and two females entered. Girls or women, it was difficult to say, probably more the former. Both would pass as attractive and wore skirts that – in some circles – would be classed as inappropriate. Both wore their hair long, in one case shoulder-length, the other – blond waves tossed a quarter of the way to the slimmest of waif-like waists.

For an instant the pair halted by the door, a quick overview as if to establish the place's credentials before venturing arm-in-arm across the floor, placing themselves on stools some four feet to the right of Maximus-Plus who made his own quick reconnoitre of the new arrivals settling into place on his right. As a gesture of conviviality he raised the bottle, watching as the nearest one nudged her friend, urging her to take a glance to her left. He disposed of a little more of the bottle's contents and replaced it on the bar.

It was upon the arrival of drinks that the girls drew into the first of a series of huddles, the blonde one, the nearest one, emerging moments later, shifting fractionally to her left.

'Alright?' she said, the enquiry levelled directly at Maximus-Plus.

Maximus-Plus turned, first identifying the source of the voice and subsequently acknowledging the enquiry with a raising of bottle to lips.

Which prompted the second one, the furthest one, to take her turn to lean across.

'You 'ere on your own?' Both girls stared – each as eager as the other not to be excluded from the answer. Maximus-Plus turned to face them.

'I am unaccompanied – yes.'

The girls exchanged more looks. One of them – the shoulder-length haircut one – leant closer.

'We were just sayin'. The music's a bit loud.'

As if in illustration of the point, she raised her voice, leaning across to make a point of encroaching on her friend's territory. Piped music had dominated proceedings since their arrival. Two hands were placed on top of the bar and Maximus-Plus turned again to face the girls.

'Yes, it is.'

The blonde girl's glass was poised within touching distance of lips.

Maximus-Plus's superbly-quaffed features continued to come under scrutiny as the girls drank their vodka-tonics in relative silence. Maximus-Plus, equally quick to take advantage of the lull in proceedings, had been observing the girls' striking apparel, with its few interesting pointers – nails extending from the tips of fingers like lines of brightly coloured molluscs, the peach-cream eye shadow, deftly administered across sculpted, finely-drawn eyelids. Zoe, the nearest one, leant closer.

'I'm Zoe. And this is Michaela,' she said.

Maximus-Plus raised the bottle and tilted it towards his lips. 'I am Maximus-Plus,' he said, angling the bottle and extending a hand.

Obliged to accept the hand, Zoe extended her hand; it felt limp and weak; she wasn't accustomed to shaking people's hands. At the release of hands Michaela – not wishing to be seen as missing out – leant across.

'What's that? Max what?'

Maximus-Plus turned to her and repeated his name, replacing the bottle on the counter.

The girls exchanged looks and Michaela did a quick reconnoitre. He appeared to be on his own, no girl in sight, or any mates as far as she could make out. She shifted in her seat. 'Ask him if he's meeting anyone,' she urged, seeking to take advantage of Zoe's closer proximity.

'No...' Zoe was adamant. No way was she going to act as a go-between, not even for her best friend. 'You ask him.' Zoe was back to her vodka-and-tonic. 'He said he's on his own...'

'He said *now* – he didn't say about later!'

'Alright...' Michaela leaned grumpily across her friend's shoulder, seeking to catch Max's eye.

'You 'ere on your own then?' she asked, turning up the volume as justification for having to repeat the question.

Maximus-Plus responded with a three-quarter turn and two deft flicks of the forehead.

'My name is Maximus-Plus and as I stated earlier, I am here alone – yes.'

As a salutary gesture, he raised the bottle, excusing himself as he proceeded to withdraw a Smart-phone from a pouch at his side and begin tapping into the buttons. For a while the girls contented themselves in the role of passive observers, watching Maximus-Plus tend to his business, until, moments later, he replaced the phone with another quick flick of the forehead and a smile, revealing two lines of perfectly aligned teeth.

In due course more drinks were ordered, MP informing them at some length that this one would be on him. Though intrigued to be passing time with one so young and apparently unaccounted for, the girls were beginning to find it a struggle keeping up with him. He seemed to have found an extra gear from somewhere, coming out with words and expressions that – at first hearing – were difficult to grasp. Zoe wanted to check she'd got his name right. She leant across.

'What did you say your name was?' Maximus-Plus repeated it raising the bottle from the bar. It was Michaela's turn to speak. 'I ain't being funny or nothing, but it's a strange name.'

Under different circumstances Zoe might have leapt at her friend. But secretly, she'd been thinking along similar lines. Maximus-Plus turned to explain. 'The name stems from a bastardisation of the striving for absolute truth. The *Plus* is a patent – a kind of brand-name.'

The girls nodded, Zoe seeming bemused.

'I like your teeth,' she said.

'Acrylic, high-tech amalgam with hints of titanium,' Maximums-Plus explained, with a few further flicks of the forehead – indication of a few million more gigabytes settling into place somewhere behind the scenes. The response was immediate: the hair acquiring a more spiky texture, the eyes sharper and more jagged under the reflections of light, the lips swelling with their absorption of specially-convened liner-cells. He turned, catching Zoe mid-gulp of a shot of vodka-tonic.

'You too have a number of engaging features.' Though directed at Zoe, the observation might easily have been levelled at either of them. Zoe blushed and looked down as Maximus-Plus went on to elaborate.

'Your eyes – two pearl droplets, the lips – two rose petals, soft on the eye and no doubt gentle to the touch...' The words coming thick and fast, if not entirely within his control.

'Thankyou,' said Zoe, stifling a giggle and turning to her friend as some compensation for the fact that she wasn't the one being complimented.

A hand extended in the direction of Zoe's top.

'And the top.' A finger slid against and under the collar, slightly exposing the pink flesh. 'Lovely tassel effect at the bridge of the sleeve.' Zoë reached for the tufts of her top, pulling at them to exaggerate their puffiness.

'Thankyou,' she said again, placing careful emphasis on each syllable and brushing herself down even more self-consciously.

MP's eyes lingered a moment, taking in the curve of her shoulder, the tiny cup-cake breasts and the pencil-thin waist perched precariously on the chrome-legged stool. He took another drink and replaced the bottle on the bar, reaching to brush a hand across the black quaff approaching completion across the bridge of his skull, smiling profusely.

Zoe was getting pissed and was wondering if Maximus-Plus was getting pissed too. He ought to be the amount he'd stuck away but with him you could never tell. She'd been watching him since the moment they'd been alone but without wishing to make it too obvious – the way he sat stiffly in his seat, constantly peering round – appearing to take everything in but reacting to virtually nothing beyond the occasional flick of his forehead and a strange ticking noise coming from somewhere inside his chest, or the odd aside to Zoe: some observation on the highlights in her hair or the puffy effect in her top. All routine stuff, and no way geared to revealing what he was actually thinking, or – what his plans might be for later. Either way, Zoe was hooked. As far as she was concerned he could easily have walked straight out of *My Guy*. In fact the more pissed she got, the better-looking he seemed to get which was stupid she knew, but somehow it just seemed that way. She loved his hair. It had gone all black and spiky – like a baby hedgehog. She wanted to reach up and brush her fingers against it; she wondered if he'd mind. Somehow she got the feeling he wasn't the type who'd welcome someone running their fingers through his hair.

Her curiosity had not gone unnoticed. Maximus-Plus too had been far from idle when it came to observing his neighbour's mannerisms: watching her shift repeatedly back and forth on her seat, ostensibly reaching for something in her bag but more subtle messages registering amongst the application-files of the CPU.

It was with astute sense of timing that he ventured to meet her, gripping her hand, brushing the five digits against his palm and clamping them firmly in his own.

There was a moment's hesitation before she allowed herself to be drawn closer, their lips meeting for the first time, Zoe's arm rising to cradle his neck.

She purred gently at the parting of lips. Maximus-Plus smiled, baring lines of crystal-white teeth and gripping Zoe's hand firmly in his.

With the preliminaries done and dusted and Michaela having made her excuses and departed some time ago, the pair sat for a while, Maximus-Plus content to observe the various scenarios beginning to take shape around him, whilst allowing an arm to drift periodically across what were unquestionably the slimmest shoulders he'd encountered for some time. Zoe shuffled closer, her own hand tinkering tentatively along the platinum hairs of Maximus-Plus's forearm.

It was a few vodkas-and-tonics later and following repeated glances at his watch that Maximus-Plus leant to whisper something, allowing time for Zoe to finish her drink before drawing her to her feet and with a few further words in her ear, ushering her slightly wobbly exit through the door and out on the street – his manner firm yet far from insistent.

Once on the street, he gripped her hand more tightly and led her equally firmly past the hustle and bustle of late-night revellers; the sushi-bars, the coffee-shops – all swishing in and out of vision as he steered the pair of them past one doorway after another, finally reaching a dimly-lit corner where – as if by prior arrangement – a cab stood ready and waiting.

Only the grim light of the hallway illuminated their ascent to the third floor. Zoe had been the one to extend the invitation.

Knowing Janis would be home and Tanya and her boyfriend gave some grounds for security and she wasn't up for going back to his place, not yet. Not that he'd suggested it, in fact he'd hardly said anything about where he lived or what he did or anything about himself at all, which was a bit strange, but some blokes were like that, a bit secretive. Maybe he had something to hide. She hoped so! She giggled; she was definitely getting pissed.

The kettle was filled and Zoe was feeling good. She sensed Maximus-Plus was feeling good too though you could never be sure what he was thinking. He was definitely a bit odd: the strange expressions he came out with, the sudden flicks of his forehead and the peculiar ticking sounds coming from somewhere inside his chest. He'd hardly said a word since they'd left the bar. She'd thought he maybe *was* a bit shy, like he was hiding something from her, which – at that moment, just the two of them alone together in the kitchen – she thought was quite sweet.

And there were no complaints a few moments later when, as she turned from the counter bearing two mugs, he edged forward, taking the mugs from her grasp and placing them on the counter.

She allowed herself to be kissed, succumbing to his technique of spearing her lips with the tip of his tongue and reaming it back and forth across the bridge of her mouth. She drew back, finally allowing herself to ruffle fingers through the now fully-matured thatch of bristly hair.

'Max.' There was hesitation as she breathed his name, unsure how he'd react to the use of the abbreviation. She looked up, meeting the glassy stare with slightly distended lips. 'Can I call you Max – do you mind?'

Maximus-Plus broke off for a moment.

'Of course not…You must access whatever term springs to mind; there's no call for inhibitions when it comes to nights out with Maximus-Plus.' He retreated slightly, seeking to share a moment's amusement in his use of the third-person.

Zoe thanked him, closing her eyes and – under his close supervision – led the way to the landing.

Ideally positioned – side by side on the duvet, he aligned himself stiffly alongside her.

The procedure from hereon would likely be straightforward: having settled her on her haunches, a timed exploration of the upper torso would be followed by a more leisurely focus in and around the lumbar region. He watched Zoe's head keel back, small bubbles beginning to appear across the line of her lips.

Within minutes his trousers, shirt and undergarments and Zoe's blouse, skirt and underwear were stacked neatly at their side.

A finger-tip exploration of the mid-sternum was followed by feather-light touches of the tongue, a familiar route towards – and then in and around – the upper, then lower, pudendum area. Time, he knew, was key; nothing would be left to chance. He looked up, able to observe Zoe's head twitch from side to side accompanied by a series of drawn-out sighs.

'Max.' He watched too, the gentle parting of her thighs – a far-from-unusual development even at this stage – inviting a gentle probing of the naval valley and upper femoral flanks. The count-down continued, the area proving particularly responsive...only forty to fifty seconds before the call to switch to their more celebrated protrusions above: in Zoe's case, tiny peaks but with a singularly sculpted areola surrounding the nipples: vaguely Egyptian-looking unless he was much mistaken. A little exploratory fondling – a few tweaks and pulls – culminated in vice-like grips of the teeth on the now fully distended tips.

All appeared to be in order: Zoe clenched the duvet, her breath coming in a series of short sharp bursts.

Again timing was paramount: a finger-tip circumlocution of the labial lips followed by a single, then double and finally triple fingered – up-to-the-knuckle – insertion of the vaginal tract.

'Max!' Zoe found herself bucking to meet his feverishly working fingers.

'Max...Max!'

Re-aligning himself, he withdrew his fingers and in a split-second manoeuvre, introduced his chrome-domed appendage, which, after a few minor adjustments, slipped with ease into Zoe's well-lubricated tract, programmed to brush at two second intervals against the semi-concealed stalk at the labial apex.

It was familiar territory: a measured insertion, a few superbly-timed thrusts of the buttocks – and the girl beneath him beginning to go crazy.

'Max – Max.' Max drove on – the switch to default-mode timing fruition at somewhere in the region of eighty to ninety seconds. The girl could talk all she wanted.

'Max...' she breathed. 'Its – It's never been like this before.'

Zoe was on the brink. Maximus-Plus too, was close. But it was Zoe who led the way, launching into a series of spasms and sinking her teeth into the corner of an already dishevelled duvet, as – moments later – a few feet above her, Maximus-Plus shuddered, heaved and jettisoned some two to three million gigabytes into the base of her cervix.

'Max...Max!' Maximus-Plus released what remained of the ejaculatory cycle and collapsed onto the pillow – arms folded across the crumpled duvet.

It was another special moment, a little more controlled on this occasion – yet still ample opportunity to regain composure and assimilate appropriate data.

'Orgasm' he knew, was the label most commonly ascribed. He'd heard the term floated on a number of occasions. And, again, it appeared to have worked a treat. Certainly a preferred option than the 'faking it' route adopted by some – more typically females by all account – a topic of many a lively conversation on a girls' night out.

Zoe too lay exhausted against the pillow, her slim frame rising and falling in time with Maximus-Plus's rib-cage, watching as he blew on his fingers in an attempt to restore some feeling to the joints.

'Max.' She breathed the word lightly, reluctant to disturb the air of contentment that had drifted over the pair of them.

'No-one's ever...done me like that.' She squirmed closer, picking her words carefully, allowing an arm to flop an arm across Maximus-Plus's midriff. 'You know – knowing exactly *what* to do...and *when* to do it.'

She sighed and popped a kiss on the bridge of his upper scapula.

Maximus-Plus pulled the duvet across his shoulders.

'Well.' He paused a moment, doing his usual impression of thinking it over before presenting her with an explanation. 'Most blokes aren't so adept at facilitating data and decoding it to maximum effect.'

Zoe nodded and stirred a finger across his perfectly-formed rib-cage.

'They don't know nothing – most blokes,' she sighed, curling her arm across the spidery hairs of his chest, a finger brushing lightly against the skin.

'Maximising opportunity,' he said, looking across. 'And – educating ones-self.'

He awarded her a knowing look. 'That's the key Zoe. Assimilating available data – it's really no great secret.' He smiled and turned to face her, their lips meeting briefly, Zoe's head resting lightly on his chest. As far as she could recall, it was the first time he'd used her name.

'Access time!' he announced with a few flicks of his forehead and making a few final adjustments to his watch. Zoe drew closer.

'Mmm,' she said, purring contentedly – the banks of hard-drives and colossal wads of memory cunningly concealed behind Maximus-Plus's more than presentable exterior currently on-hold – and for a while at least, seeming set to remain so.

Zoe shifted closer, the strange ticking noise inside his chest suddenly little more than a resounding heartbeat.

Exhibit 149

'Okay listen.' The teacher had them lined up in twos, on the left, out of the general line of traffic but able to hear her instructions as far as the back. 'At the back – can you hear?' Confirmation arrived in muffled grunts and vague nodding of heads.

'Just remember...You're representing the school; you're on-show. As Mr. Davis says, to those of you who bother to listen in assembly, '*You* are the school'. A pause followed – time enough for the gravity of the observation to register.

Each child held a bag containing a gallery-plan, pen, pencil, coloured pencils, the worksheet to be completed: partly during the trip and partly for tonight's homework, to be handed in tomorrow, a packed-lunch, a bottle of drink, preferably not fizzy.

When they were ready and quiet, which wasn't immediately, they were led by a teacher leading from the front, making their way, in twos, past a man with his left half cut away and his innards showing, to the doors, where they stopped at a point beneath a *Light Captured Through The Ages* display pinned to the wall next to a bronze statue of a unicorn. The teacher looked at her watch.

'Right – first we stick together, no talking during the talk; you listen and you can ask questions. Later – during lunch – you'll have 'free time' to go to the toilet, go to the shop, don't spend *all* your money on sweets. Go to the canteen...talk to your neighbour. Now...'

Bags were placed on the floor and worksheets clipped to the school's clip-boards. Once formed into a rough semi-circle, their attention was drawn to questions 1 – 10 to be completed during

Exhibit 149

the first part of the tour. The teacher had them look up, waving a hand in the general direction of 1 – 6. On confirmation all was clear, they were directed to questions 7 – 10 to be completed in their groups during the 'free-time' after the tour and for homework.

John looked only fleetingly at the worksheet, the surrounding hall seeming a more engaging proposition: its whiteness and sense of space reminding him of a film he'd seen about Heaven, where and a man climbs stairs to try and get there but keeps getting interrupted. Everywhere you looked faces seemed to be staring back at you: frozen expressions peering into space or the eyes of earnest onlookers.

They were led, in twos, to the left rear side of the hall, to the side of a bronze statue. From there they would follow a route round the perimeter of the first room, completing questions 1 to 3, 4-7 to follow later, and then 8 – 10 on pages 3 and 4.

The teacher stopped a moment allowing them all time to catch their breath before taking up a position against the wall, and when they were quiet, indicating the first picture pinned over her left shoulder – drawing their attention to the colours, to count how many they saw, as in *actually* saw, as opposed to just how many were in the picture. She glanced over her shoulder taking her own quick stab at the answer, allowing a moment for them to write their answers in the space provided.

On to the next picture: a series of concentric circles appearing to rotate simultaneously but in diametrically opposed directions – moving in, out – and around in a way devised to confuse the link between eye and brain. They were told to look at it for five seconds and write the answer quickly and without having to dwell on it for too long, and not to worry about spellings.

A few yards beyond that – *Gyro Shapes For A New Millennium* was an arrangement of multi-coloured chains constructed around a prism which appeared to hang in mid-air. They answered the question and drew one of the chains. An attendant, weary of forever hovering on the brink of all the action, stepped forwards to inform them it was likely an interpretation of a throwback to the Egyptian Abydos with a link to the mortuary temple of Seti. The teachers thanked him and said it was up to them when the children asked if they had to write it down.

Once they'd finished drawing their chains it was five minutes 'free-time': no wandering from the room and no going too near the exhibits, just the chance to sit on one of the seats at the side and, if they wished, to colour in the pictures on pages two and three or add some touches to the pictures they'd just done, whilst the teachers amused themselves walking round to see how many had copied 'Millennium' correctly.

When time was up they moved to the next room where, for the first exhibit in line, they had to count the dots. Did anyone know a quick way of doing it? Jennifer Mayhew said to count up one side and then count across the top and do a times sum. She was commended and awarded a *merit*, to be recorded in her planner later, during lunch. Did they all understand *why* that was a quick way of doing it? Some did.

Next was a line of pictures along the end wall entitled *Countrified Excursions Based On An Exoneration Of Time*. They wrote the title, and then worked their way in twos along the line, noting the greenness of the fields and the use of bold colours to highlight the flowers...magnolia, crocuses – some larger than the gate at the front, and finally, the sky: in two of the pictures a thick royal blue rather like Chelsea's football kit. And then the clouds – depicted as wads of cotton-wool dotting the skyline from one print to the next. They wrote their answers and looked again to try and spot the link. A few questions followed: what was the thing near the gate at the edge of the field? No-one could be absolutely sure. They wrote down what they thought it might be or failing that just left it blank.

John stared hard at the sun, and the sky and the colours. He wrote what he saw or thought he saw or might have seen, and wrote something no-one else could see. As Damien Entwistle pointed out, you can write anything you want for that.

EXHIBIT 149

The next room had brightly coloured cubes and rectangles and fuzzy shapes attached to the corners. They looked closely and did some counting and drawing. Underneath was a playpen where you could arrange fuzzy cubes in the way you wanted and attach them to fuzzy felt clouds. They would need to take turns which meant forming two teams: team A building their 'cloud-boxes' whilst team B went to the toilet, and then swapping over.

John was more interested in going to the toilet than making his cloud-boxes. On his return he saw a sign that warned against getting too close to the exhibits or taking photographs. The teacher saw him and warned him against wandering too far and getting too close.

Next stop was a room to the right where a huge chrome ball was floating in a shallow well. They wrote the title *Ball Floating In Well* and answered the question. They were allowed to stir the ball and make it rotate under pressure if they wanted to, but they had to go one at a time and take care their hands didn't slip sending them toppling into the well.

After filling in the plan of the two rooms – conveniently completing two of this month's Geography targets in the process – it was lunch.

When they were ready were they led, in twos, to what was called *The Esplanade* – a central area featured clearly on their plan: a small courtyard – a mini play-are with an ice-cream stall and counter from the souvenir shop.

It was a hot and busy place; kids from seemingly every borough in the city buzzing with excitement at the suspension of customary routine, tiny-tots higgledy-piggledy midst the raucous shouts of older children.

John finished his crisps and crumpled the bag, depositing it and his other debris in the nearby receptacle.

It was hot – too hot sitting in the sun. He squinted at the scene stretching to the far side of the patio: kids of all creeds and colours heading pell-mell for the ice-cream stall, crowding each other's space and toppling exuberantly onto piles of fellow pupils, deliberately pulling each other away and then joining the fray in their own animated exhibitions of friendship and rudimentary attempts at courtship. Whilst lines of Asian girls watched passively from the sidelines – sedately sharing crisp bags and plastic lunch-boxes; the whole performance laid on free-of-charge and reaching as far as the *The Esplanade*'s perimeter of concrete blocks and multi-coloured mosaics.

His eyes drifted from the main players to the souvenir-shop to the concrete blocks, scouring the scene for any chink in the day's armour: any feasible means of escape. There was a door at the far side, a solid-looking glass door with a sign above it. A side beyond the main quadrangle they hadn't yet visited and, according to the plan they'd been given, were unlikely to get to. Certainly a quieter-looking part of the building than the side they'd been in. And no-one had said anything about having to remain in *The Esplanade* during lunch. It was free-time; they only knew they needed to be back beside the bronze statue at one-o-clock.

He upped himself unobtrusively from his seat, making a point of milling with the throngs whilst taking regular glances over his shoulder lest he be reprimanded for wandering too far or endangering his, or others', safety. Once beyond the focal point he stepped up the pace, pausing only when he reached the door and with a last glance across the square, pushed it open and disappeared inside.

It was the coolness that struck him first; that, and an overwhelming sense of silence. He stood his ground, taking a moment to convince himself he hadn't ventured into alien territory, making a point of sticking close to the wall, his every move scrutinised by eyes peering from deep-set mahogany frames. He took a step further. As far as he could see there was no 'Forbidden Entry' sign in either direction.

At the end of the corridor lines of silver mosaics were pinned behind glass frames, ahead of which, illuminated on its own little slab – a huge box, white on one side and black on the other, looking a little out of place in its tailor-made bed of gravel.

Exhibit 149

He read the sign that accompanied it...*Both Sides Now* and then followed a sign that led him to a longer corridor.

One end was sectioned off by ropes, which meant a right turn, at the end of which another room came into view, a small room that appeared to have been latched on, almost as an afterthought: a room that, as he got closer, reminded him of the waiting-room at the clinic: small, neat, flooded in light from a strategically positioned glass-panelled roof, casting the whole area like a children's play-area in a nursery school.

Maybe it was the light that drew him in, or maybe another light – a tiny blue light seeping from the corner of a huge glass box stuck in the centre of the room. He crept closer and looked at the sign. It said only...*Exhibit 149.*

He peered through the glass.

Placed on the floor in the centre of the box was a pig's head, a *real* pig's head as far as he could make out – severed and pink and leathery-looking – its expression glazed and quite unabashed at having been detached from the remainder of its body and stuck in the middle of the floor, left with little option than to return people's stares from deep, avuncular eyes – its first audience for maybe days, weeks...months!

He looked closer. Then it struck him the pig wasn't alone; fellow-occupants – scores, hundreds, maybe thousands of flies buzzed and hammered round him, skirting the box's perimeter and gathering en-masse for renewed assaults on the panes of glass. Whilst others, more resigned to their fate, lay on the ground sleeping-off the pig's secretions, waiting for their number to come up – to take their turn on one of four tubes arranged in a rack beneath a bright blue light – to be frizzled to the next clump – and to finally drop onto the ever-increasing pile beneath.

No need for questions or filling in spaces on a worksheet; no oscillating-patterns, fluffy clouds or fuzzy boxes; just a dead pig, flies, and the certainty of death – the only thing that had made any *real* sense all day.

It was as fly number three-hundred-and-twenty-four for the day was settling into position on the wire that a voice broke from the rear of the room.

'John Aldwick. What on earth are you doing here?'

He stood back from the box but didn't bother to look behind or attempt to answer the voice. He knew a rhetorical question when he heard one. The teacher did the looking-back for him. 'Come away. That's nothing to do with us. We're nothing to do with this part of the building. You're not allowed here. You should be eating your lunch, visiting the shop, talking to your neighbour and be back in the room by the bronze statue at one-o-clock, the one next to where we started.'

She was stood by the entrance, waiting. 'Come away – now.'

He reluctantly retreated. He'd guessed all along that they weren't supposed to be in this part of the building, but there hadn't been any signs. The teacher followed him from the room. Behind him the show would go on: a few flies biding their time over a pile of pig's gristle, the promise of an early grave just round the corner – all under the watchful eye of a cathode-ray lamp glowing as fiercely and defiantly as the day it was born. The only direction left to him was the one by which he had come.

At one-o-clock promptly they were assembled by the bronze statue in time for afternoon register. He joined the line, taking the worksheet from his bag.

Only when they were ready were they led single-file to take their places around the perimeter of a neighbouring room for what was likely destined to be the highlight of the day:

First, an opportunity to take in a giant mural covering all four sides of the room, complete with green fields and a dazzling array of flowers, from hyacinth to daffodil from tiny crocuses to giant explosions of colour cast against small woodland paths and a garden-gate superimposed on a water-colour background.

The instructions came via an off-the-scenes microphone; a warning for everyone to stand well back.

EXHIBIT 149

Teachers and children alike gathered at the far side of the room, watching and waiting until, moments later, a shutter was released and a deluge of butterflies: scores, hundreds – maybe thousands – were unleashed into the room. Children squealed and clapped hands as the exquisite creatures fluttered and cascaded in and around the backdrop of flowers and five-barred gate that was the entrance to a farm. Arms reached out, making half-hearted grabs at the flapping wings in the hope of cradling one in tiny palms, if only for a few seconds.

John watched from the side. It was certainly an impressive sight. Yet, as is often the case in these things, no sooner had it begun to gather pace than someone saw fit to bring it to an abrupt end. Responding to some behind-the-scenes signal – and to the tune of much protest – the butterflies were hauled back to base behind trap-doors in readiness for the next show in about fifteen minutes time. The children watched and waved and then turned their attention to completing their answers and turning to the last page to follow the final instructions.

In a neighbouring room they took their seats to complete the final question – picking the exhibit that had made the biggest impression, and saying why. The teachers could guess the most likely answers.

John contemplated an answer, but couldn't think what to write.

Oscillating-circles, fuzzy boxes, garden gates, hordes of cavorting butterflies...the choice seemed endless – but somehow they all seemed to miss the point.

He put his pen away and joined the queue to board the coach. At the end of the day it just meant he'd get a few less marks.

The Strange Tale Of Hollie's Amazing Diminishing Dad

The afternoon was drawing to its close as Hollie, wearying a little from her Game-Boy, turned to her mother, still busy with her ironing at the far side of the room.

'Mum, daddy's really getting quite small now isn't he?' she said, placing the gadget to one side for a moment and looking up to face her mother.

Her mother forced a smile, whilst focusing her attention on removing the crease in the blouse splayed open across the board.

'Yes dear he is. Very much so, in fact.'

Her daughter continued to look up.

'It *is* strange isn't it for a man daddy's size to get to be as small as that.'

The observation – unspectacular though it was – prompted her mother to press more urgently into the garment's sleeve. The fact was, they'd gone through it with her a number of times, but like most kids her age, it was likely no easy thing to come to terms with, hence the need to bring it out in the open from time to time, if only to gain a little attention.

Their mother looked across.

'It was something he drank at work dear, or at least that's what we think.'

'Bio-Cellular Reducing Agent,' put in Jake, her brother, busily scrolling the pages of his BlackBerry or whatever it was at the far side of the room. 'Part of his new dietary-plan.'

His mother swept the garment to one side and reached for a pair of socks. Her daughter looked up.

'What's that?'

Her mother laid the first sock across the board and steadied the iron above it.

'A name they use for a solution dear that your father was working on at work – to do with his research into cell diminution in small rodents and tiny mammals – clear – effervescent – devoid of taste. We think he might have drunk it instead of his Sparkling Spring Water. The glasses were side by side on the counter.'

Her daughter, seeming a little bewildered, looked up.

'But wasn't that a bit of a silly thing to do?' she asked, still of a mind to make something of an issue of it.

'Yes,' put in her brother, without the need for any prompting, and still speaking from the far side of the room.

Her mother reached for the second sock.

'Well – yes – if you look at it one way – pragmatically. But you must remember it was an easy mistake to make. Both solutions being clear, relatively tasteless, and in similar shaped glasses next to each other on the counter.'

Her son, Jake was saying nothing. He'd made his position clear: that, if it turned out to be true, they'd be in a position to sue the company, which, coupled with his numerous insurance policies, would be no mean reckoning. His mother had pointed out there'd be time for such things in due course. For the time being, the last thing any of them needed, particularly their father, was to make any unnecessary fuss; to remember that they were a normal family doing normal family things – the only point being that their father was rapidly getting smaller.

And getting smaller – he certainly was....

Fact was they'd barely clapped eyes on him over the last day or so, when – quite out of the blue – the door swung open open, and there he was – framed in the jamb, about the same height as the plug sockets on the wall, arms like two long feelers reaching out from the cuffs of his shoulders; his head...almost like a pumpkin – wisps of hair drifting from a few lingering spots like tiny feathers.

As their mother had hinted, it *had* been a quite cataclysmic turn of events: doubly so, picking up, as it did, on his recent ground-breaking discoveries in chromatin-diminution and repression of genes in pariental cellular structure in small animals – mainly rodents – with plans to infiltrate the serum in the haemoglobin of small mammals. That it should be brought home to such devastating effect was something none of them could have bargained for.

For what seemed an eternity he stood calmly surveying the scene, watching the family observe *him* – until, tiring perhaps from being a constant source of attention, he made a quick bee-line for his seat...only to find it was like facing the first leg of some giant obstacle-course. Fortunately Hollie was on hand to link her arms round his chest and hoik him into place – his little legs wriggling and thrashing around over the edge of the cushion.

Having announced his arrival and shuffled himself into place, he seemed content to sit a while, sniffling quietly, taking stock of the scene of activity, or inactivity, around him, to the tune of a few growling noises and a series of high-pitched yelps emanating from somewhere in the base of his throat.

His wife reached for the next shirt and, looking up briefly, laid the damp sleeve along the tapered end of the board. She at least managed a smile. Having her family round her like this had become something of a rarity: her son draped across the chair at the far side of the room, forever flicking a wad of hair from his eyes and noodling with the buttons on his MP3 player or BlackBerry or whatever it was. And perched on the settee opposite, her daughter, Hollie – growing up fast; ten years old and with a recently acquired habit of peering dolefully through strands of bedraggled hair – an imitation of her mother's jet-black, or as her husband sometimes saw it – Satanic-look.

And, of course, her husband – perched on the seat opposite, currently twiddling with the clasp that held his troos in place, and looking – midst a pool of light from the corner standard-lamp – like some homunculus monkey clad in his tiny braces and bold-patterned Action-Man top.

She smiled, and turning the shirt, extended the second sleeve along the curve of the board.

On the far side of the room, her husband finally seemed to have got himself organised. Sitting bolt upright in his seat awarded him the opportunity to, at least, *feel* part of the action, convince himself that he still had some part to play, if only as spectator – watching the iron slide back and forth across Hollie's school-blouse, his son tapping away on his mobile or whatever it was, and his daughter weaving back and forth on her seat, staring at him through strands of dishevelled hair.

As ever, it was Hollie who'd had been first to catch his eye. She thought he looked *really* cute, particularly in the bright scarlet braces that came over his shoulders to keep the troos in place, and the tiny pouch strapped round his tummy to keep his goodies in. He returned the look, his tiny nostrils flaring a little under the crimson light creeping under the lampshade as he appeared to reach for something stashed in the belt beneath him.

It was Conference-Time – one of the family's twice weekly get-togethers in the lounge to share experiences and for them to fill their father in on what was happening at school and with their friends and Hollie with her piano lessons and Jake with his web-site that was forever failing to get off the ground, and for reasons that were – forever – beyond his control. Though 'Conference' was, by now, something of a misnomer, being little more than the dissemination of a few facts – their father able to take-on-board what was said, but able to offer little by way of response beyond a few growls and the occasional high-pitched yelp.

Yet – even at this stage all was not lost: there were moments that seemed to transcend the need to have these things verbalised; like now, for instance – watching him reach down inside his bum-bag to extract what appeared to be a document and promptly hoist in the air as if urging it to be taken and investigated more closely.

At first, there were no takers – just an exchange of looks; their mother biting her tongue and pressing more urgently on the sleeve of the blouse, Jake twiddling more fiercely at the buttons on his lap, no-one seeming particularly eager to take up the invitation to examine the document, or whatever it was, more closely.

It was down to Hollie – who liked surprises, particularly when they came wrapped in glossy pictures – to rise from her seat to take what appeared to be a tiny booklet from her father's grasp.

It *was* a booklet; comprising a number of folded sheets, stapled in the middle. Their father had clearly been a busy bee up there in his little room.

The question was...doing what? Having time on your hands isn't *necessarily* a good thing, the family could vouch for that. Their father, apt to dwell on things at the best of times, had always been a stickler for coming up with 'answers' to what he regarded as the Big questions: *Who* we are...*What* we are...just what it all means in terms of the Bigger picture; indeed – just what the future *does* hold – for any of us. On this occasion he appeared to have gone into some kind of overdrive – producing what appeared to be a mini story-book littered with illustrations.

Hollie held the book aloft.
'Look – daddy's written a story,' she said, waving the document from side to side.

His wife looked up fleetingly from her ironing and Jake temporarily diverted his gaze from his MP3 player or BlackBerry.

Their father sat back purring contentedly – the occasional high-pitched yelp the only interruption to the scene of domesticity around him.

It appeared to be an adventure story. The cover had a loathsome-looking creature wielding what looked like a toothpick at another slightly larger creature, against a blurred backdrop of twigs and what appeared to be bits of a forest.

Hollie loved stories. She settled back in her seat, her thumb placed firmly in her mouth, to set about devouring it from cover to cover.

And quite a story it was! All about a man – who gets smaller and smaller, until, one day, he finally disappears into the carpet where he finds himself surrounded by lots of other miniscule creatures – all living in the depths of the carpet. At first, he finds himself having to fend off some of the bigger creatures bearing a weapon made of a splinter of wood. But vanquishing the foe – and in such valiant fashion immediately makes him a hit amongst the other creatures and before long he becomes their *leader* – teaching them how to make weapons and protect themselves – showing them how to do things and lead more useful lives! There were pictures too: of one of the 'carpet creatures' brandishing a spear and then one standing on a box, pointing a finger, talking to them all about how they can lead more useful lives.

Hollie clapped hands and held the book in the direction of her mother, eager to have her come and share in the story's secrets.

But her mother was still busy with her ironing and would look later. Jake was also busy. On hearing the gist of the story, he wanted to know why one of the bigger creatures hadn't come along and gobbled him up before he'd had time to arm himself.

But Hollie remained undeterred. She liked the story. She loved make-believes and fantasies and closing the book and holding it at distance, peered approvingly at the cover, slipping from her seat to step across and give her father a big hug.

Her father was beaming too, and pointing: first at himself, then down at the carpet and finally at the book still clutched tightly in Hollie's hand, growling and finally yelping with such ferocity it almost had Hollie leaping out of her skin.

'Yes...I know...You're a clever daddy,' she said, giving him another hug and leaping back into her seat.

'Ah...bless him...' she said, examining the cover once more and finally placing it to one side.

She'd already decided to take the story to school to ask the teacher if she could read it to the little children: the infants or maybe the reception class. They loved stories like this. And when she'd read it they could draw their own pictures; pretending it was their daddy fending off the carpet-creatures and then making friends with them.

Their mother laid the next garment to one side, as Jake flicked the hair from his eyes and, for once, looked up from his screen.

It was shortly after, that their father – perhaps tiring from all the excitement and having observed his family going about their business long enough – finally slid from his chair to trot his way back across the carpet, booklet in hand.

The family turned – Hollie waving wildly through strands of bedraggled hair, his wife placing the iron to one side to watch him trot his way back to the door. At which point he stopped and looked back, flexing the braces and taking a final overview of the scene he was abandoning. With a few throaty growls and a final parting yelp, he turned, and, seconds later – disappeared from view.

It was as he turned to the door that Jake, revolving in his seat, levelled the BlackBerry in his father's direction, holding it inches from his eye.

'Evidence,' he announced – grabbing his shot and taking a quick glance at the result on the screen – the up-and-coming insurance claims never far from his thoughts.

The week that followed, though largely uneventful in many respects, saw their father continue to diminish, until, by the end of the week, he was roughly the size of a large rat, barely able to see, and able to utter little beyond near-inaudible squeaks. Virtually all attempts at communication had been abandoned though Hollie would occasionally lie on the floor, place her ear next to his wispy face, and fill him in on a few bits of gossip, but beyond a few whispery squeaks, she got little back. The Conferences had been abandoned. In their place...'Evening Get-Togethers': a chance to sit on the sofa with a cup of tea and a biscuit and watch their father scurrying back and forth across the carpet as if searching for scraps or tiny insects, after which

Hollie would perch him on her knee patting him and stroking his tiny jump-suit – made from cutting one of the fingers from a pair of kitchen gloves.

It was six days later, at approximately half-past five in the afternoon that their father finally became invisible to the naked eye: no fuss, no warning.....

Hollie had been keeping tabs on him for a while – particularly over the last day or so when he was down to thumb-nail size – and on the previous evening had taken him from the mantelpiece – easing him back and forth in his little match-box – or bedsit-flat – as their mother liked to describe it – which had been his home for a few days now.

From time to time Hollie would take the matchbox and nurse it on her knee, popping a few smidgeons of carrot-cake inside to watch her father creep along its walls and into the centre to investigate the latest 'treat' to be put before him.

It was just before five-thirty, that she leapt from her kneeling position on the floor to summon her mother, who was busy preparing tea in the kitchen.

Together, they peered down into the box. There was the hint of something happening in one of its corners – but little more. And it quickly petered out to nothing. Her mother took her daughter's hand.

Both knew what needed to happen.

There was a call upstairs, and moments later Jake appeared, hovering uneasily at the door before finally venturing closer.

With all three in position, Hollie took the box, tilted it and tapped its side a few times against the carpet, urging her father – wherever he was – to take his final steps from the world he knew – into the wide-open spaces of the carpet....

Any indication of movement was negligible. Hollie tapped the match-box a few more times to make sure – and then reached into her *Little Brown Bag* to take out what appeared to be a contraption of lolly-sticks – arranged in a square and secured at each corner to make a kind of frame.

All eyes followed as she lowered the frame to the carpet, her father by now likely established somewhere in its midst. She'd wondered about adding a few flowers, maybe a few bits of dandelion arranged to make the word – *Dad* – but her mother had quickly poo-pooed the idea, pointing out that their father wasn't into that sort of thing; that he hated making a fuss.

Even so, Hollie took the matchbox and separating the box from the lid, placed the box upside down on the fringe of the lolly-stick square with the lid next to it.

'Do you think Daddy's met any of the carpet-creatures yet?' she asked, peering deep into the Axminster pile.

Her mother managed a smile.

'I don't know dear, What do *you* think?'

Hollie thought for a moment.

'Maybe,' she said.

'Well then – *maybe*,' said her mother, squeezing her hand.

Jake was saying nothing.

Beneath them, silence ruled. Nothing moved – nothing stirred.

Moments later they turned, Hollie to take her father's storybook from the shelf, Mum to return to the kitchen where the chicken casserole was waiting to be popped into the oven. It was some time later, over tea, that Jake finally spoke up.

'I was just thinking,' he said, speaking through a mouthful of chicken and potato. 'How long do you reckon it'll be before it's okay to hoover the carpet?'

His mother spooned her smaller portion onto a waiting plate.

'About a week or two I should think,' she said.

'Three,' put in Hollie from across the table.

'Okay…two and a half,' said Jake, anxious to avoid any further ructions in the family, at least for the time being.

❦

Satisfaction

It was after making love the second time that week that my wife told me she wasn't being satisfied when we made love and never had been. I smoked a cigarette and thought about what she had said, and then watched the way she turned on her side and either drifted off to sleep or pretended to drift off to sleep. My initial reaction was...how can you drift into sleep? Then it occurred to me it could be a ploy. She was distancing herself from what she had said, possibly through annoyance or possibly to give me time to think about it and come up with a solution: give me a bit of 'breathing space', like when I was a kid and accidentally chucked a stone through a car window and immediately ran off.

I continued to smoke the cigarette and think about what my wife had said. At first I thought she was being a little mean. Not saying I didn't satisfy her, but that she'd told me and that it mattered to her.

I myself, am neither satisfied nor unsatisfied when we make love. When we have finished I dismount her and usually smoke a cigarette. I don't think it's wonderful. But I don't think it's that bad either. Which is exactly my point. Why does it matter?

After she told me I wasn't satisfying her she told me she still loved me, as if to make up for what she'd said, which was quite nice. So I told her I loved her too. Which is mainly true. Most of the time I do love her, which makes me wonder why it matters that she isn't satisfied.

I smoked a bit more. Smoking cigarettes helps me think. The reason she's told me is because she wants me to do something about it – or she wouldn't have told me. The reason she wants me to do something about it, is maybe because if I don't do something about it, she may find someone else to satisfy her.

I am thirty three and my wife is thirty six. It seems to me you can still love each other as long as both people trust each other. Smoking the cigarette got me to thinking whether *trust* is as important as being satisfied. I'd thought maybe 'trust' was more important, but maybe I was wrong. Then it occurred to me again that whilst I'm thinking about 'trust' my wife might be thinking about finding another man to satisfy her, which was – in a way – me not trusting her, so where does that leave us? They say you have to work at a marriage. I think that's right.

I watched her lying there asleep or pretending to be. She isn't what you'd call an attractive woman, I'd say she was somewhere in-between; as I think I am. I'm not handsome, but I don't think I'm ugly either. I'm not as ugly as some men I see in town. I'm not as fat as some of them either. The point being that me and my wife are suited, which is like most people. The handsome, pretty people go together, and the ordinary ones do the same, and the ugly ones too, though some of the very ugly ones don't go with anyone because a lot of people don't want to live with someone who's very ugly. The point being that no-one's perfect, and you don't have to be perfect to love someone. Whether you need to satisfy them more if they're prettier, or more handsome, I don't know. Maybe you do because if you don't someone else will step in and satisfy her, because if you're pretty, there's a lot of people waiting to do that. So I don't see why it matters that I don't satisfy my wife when we make love. The only thing I asked her was whether it makes any difference on Tuesdays, which is the other time in the week we make love. She said it didn't make any difference; I don't satisfy her on either occasion, which, thinking about it, makes sense. Perhaps it was a bit of a silly question.

After she'd told me and said she still loved me, she asked if I was alright. I said yes, mostly, but I told her I was thinking about what she'd said. She told me to try and get some sleep and pecked me on the cheek. I told her I'd try and get some sleep. First I was going to smoke another cigarette because smoking cigarettes helps me think. My wife gets annoyed when I smoke in bed because she says the smell lingers until the morning. So I'm trying to cut down.

I smoked most of the cigarette but not all of it. Smoking the cigarette made me think about whether my wife was being fair: whether it was fair to come out with it like that. I wasn't even sure what she meant. I didn't really see why she couldn't be satisfied the way things were. It got me to asking myself whether *I* was satisfied? But I couldn't come up with an answer. Coming back to my wife, I was thinking maybe it was a 'woman's thing' and maybe that's what got me thinking it might be a good idea to go to *Mave's*.

Whilst I was trying to get to sleep I wondered if there was anything different I could do when we made love; whether I should go a bit slower, or a bit quicker. If it was neither slower nor quicker it would be difficult to know what to do. I suppose I could ask her, but it isn't easy to ask your wife these sorts of things. I decided to try and get some sleep like my wife suggested. It took a while but eventually I managed it. Just before I went to sleep, I thought a bit more about my wife looking elsewhere – finding someone else to satisfy her. I don't want her to do this because it would make things very awkward and I like my wife quite a lot. Overall, I thought maybe *Mave's* would be a good idea.

Mave's is in the centre of town, not far from the pedestrian precinct, about two minutes walk from Tesco's. It's a class for men that's all about women, and you find out about it on the grapevine – not everyone knows about it. Mave keeps it quiet and insists it's men only, she prefers it that way. Maybe it's best to keep it that way.

It was about 7:15 on the next Wednesday evening when I set off to *Mave's*. We'd made love again the previous night when I'd tried moving in and out a bit quicker and a bit slower, but neither had made any difference so I knew it would be best to do something so my wife wouldn't start looking elsewhere to be satisfied.

After I'd got off the bus the walk to *Mave's* took about ten minutes.

The doorway was next to a railway siding. I went in and went to the desk where a woman smiled and asked my name. She directed me to a room at the end of the corridor and told me to walk right in because Mave didn't like the idea of you knocking on the door and having everyone look at you when you went in. The woman on the desk was a nice-looking woman. I wondered whether she was satisfied when her husband was making love to her but I didn't think it would be right to ask.

I knocked on the door and went straight in. It was smoky there, and there were lots of men – about twenty all told: men of all shapes and sizes. On the wall above the counter was a sign... *Sex for you; Sex for me; Sex is warm and sex is free* which I thought was an interesting idea.

I'd been there about thirty seconds when a woman with broad shoulders and bouncy hair like the mane of a horse came over and shook my hand. She introduced herself as Mave and said it wouldn't be long before things started to happen and to feel free to mingle a while if I wanted. She offered me a glass of wine but I don't like wine much so I said no, but thankyou for offering.

After a while she clinked a spoon against a glass and told us to sit in a circle. I wasn't sure about sitting in a circle but I was told later it was to force us to 'go public', to shed our inhibitions – being prepared to bear our souls and be open about things, which, thinking about it later, sounded quite a good thing to do.

In the circle, we had to tell everyone our name and say we were having difficulty satisfying our wives or partners. It was like what alcoholics do, except with them, it's drinking too much.

When my turn came I told everyone 'My name is Horace Harmon and I am having difficulty satisfying my wife.' Everyone was looking at me – probably because I was new and with new people you can never be sure. Then we had to turn to a partner and say it again. My partner was a thin man called Wilton Forelock who had a tendency to avoid looking at me and spoke mainly to the ground. I was hoping there wouldn't be too much to be done with partners because with Wilton it could prove to be hard work.

Mave seemed to be quite pleased with the way things had started. Next thing, she had a helper bring on a long table and place it in the middle of the circle. We all watched as the helper disappeared from the scene and the room leaving Mave with a package which she opened. Inside was what looked like a small plastic parachute which she put to one side for now.

Next, we had to tell our partners what we could remember from our sex-education lessons from school. I turned to Wilton but I couldn't remember much, if anything. I think we had to draw a diagram of a rabbit's privates, which were interesting, but I'm not sure would help in satisfying my wife. Mave told us that there was a lot of ignorance about the whole business and at one point she slapped the table, but she wasn't so much angry at us as at people – often important people – who she said were 'mental-retards' and guilty of keeping everyone (particularly men) ignorant. I wondered if it was different for women but I didn't like to ask. It was a very interesting talk and we nodded at some of the things she said. At one point I thought Wilton was in danger of dropping off to sleep and I wondered whether to nudge him to keep him awake. But then I thought it wasn't really any of my business and if he wanted to go to sleep instead of learning how to satisfy his wife maybe he should be allowed to. I don't suppose he'd be asking for his money back.

Next there was a diagram of a woman with nothing on – it was a diagram, not a picture, and she was smiling a little bit. Her privates were enlarged in another diagram to the side, so you could see the parts better. It seemed funny seeing them like that, with labels and various other bit and bobs on the chart. Mave went through the different parts of the diagram and pointed out how you could touch the different parts and said why it was important to touch the parts in a certain way. It was quite technical and to do with 'touch' and it was as much to do with each individual woman because every woman is different, which is certainly true. The next bits were a bit rude, but I knew to listen and take note. I just wasn't sure if I'd remember it all. When I asked about whether it was on a sheet she said there was a booklet to be given out at the end, which I thought was a good idea. Some of the things she said seemed a bit difficult to do or to remember to do; I'd likely need to check with the booklet to remind myself.

At the interval we were allowed to mingle and talk to each other in a relaxed fashion. I was quite glad to be able to talk to someone other then Wilton, who sat there scratching behind his ear and reading a book. One of the men, I can't remember his name, talked about him and his wife trying it doggy-style, which I thought was quite interesting though I wasn't sure what he meant, but the men chuckled and nodded so I chuckled and nodded too, but I didn't say anything. The only time I'd seen a dog doing that kind of thing was when my mother's dog used to climb on the knee of one of her church friends and mother used to reprimand it and tell it not to be so silly.

The best bit of the evening was the next bit.

Mave had us back in our seats and turned to the parachute thing at her side. It was only when she held it up that I realised it wasn't a parachute, but a plastic woman, which she blew up with a bicycle pump. I was thinking it was quite a strange thing to do, sitting there watching a plastic woman getting blown up by a bicycle pump. It didn't take long and then Mave held it up by its arms.

It was actually a quite attractive woman, even though it was made of plastic. Mave explained that women like this have come on a long way from when they were just stick-legged inflatables with a big oval mouth that seemed totally out of sync with the rest of the face. This one had a shapely body and a nice face. Strangely, even sitting and watching from a distance, I wanted to give it a name. I thought for a minute and decided to call it Candice. I wasn't sure why I chose that name, it was just the name that came to mind.

I wasn't quite sure what Candice was going to do. It couldn't speak and it couldn't move apart from when Mave held it up from side to side for us all to see. She pointed its private parts out which were a bit bigger than you'd imagine but that was likely so you could see them better.

The way she talked about the woman was very interesting – almost like it was a *real* woman. And as you listened you could almost imagine the plastic woman listening to everything and starting to speak, to join in proceedings and tell us more about her body. Which was stupid but it was a very interesting talk and there is more to blow-up plastic dolls than you might imagine. Mave described it in detail and tweaked a few bits, pulling and poking with her fingers which made some of the men giggle.

The next bit was when we had to line up behind the woman, or doll, as Mave described it, and have a go ourselves at some of the things Mave had said.

I got in the queue behind Wilton who didn't say much about the doll or look her in the eye when it was his turn. Maybe he'd seen her before. When it was my turn I had a good look at her. She was actually a quite attractive doll, even if she *was* plastic, and it was interesting doing the tweaks and bits and bobs that Mave told us to do. But – after all that – I was still a little puzzled. The doll had a nice face and a nice body and her private bits were all there. And Mave had talked about the way you can move in and out of your wife or partner, which maybe explains things a bit and got me thinking maybe you need to practise – which got me thinking of the doll. But obviously we wouldn't be taking the doll home because there were too many of us. For a moment I wondered if the idea was to take turns with it and bring it back next time but that wouldn't be a very good idea because whose to say one of us wouldn't steal it.

One of the men, standing behind me in the queue said that there would never be any trouble keeping the doll satisfied. Which was a good point and got me thinking.

When we'd finished with the doll and we'd done our last bit in the circle, I went to Mave and asked her about the doll. Then I understood. You could actually *buy* a doll just like Candice, but it could be a bit expensive. When I asked her about it she didn't mind talking about it and was pleased that part of the evening had made an impression. I asked her where you could buy the doll because if I was going to practise, I'd need to get one and I was fairly sure there were no shops in town that sold them, or at least I hadn't seen any, and she laughed and said I was damned right; you had to go to the right sort of shop – in town – which meant in London – and even then, the right part of London. Not Harrods and she laughed again. And I laughed, because I couldn't imagine buying a plastic doll from a shop like Harrods! I told her I'd like to buy a doll like this one and she thought about it a moment, and then said that we were all adults and were free to behave in whatever way we felt appropriate and let me take the number off the plastic wrapper and receipt, so that I'd hopefully get the right one. I thanked her because she'd been very helpful and I thought it would be a good idea to have a doll like Candice to practice with to help me satisfy my wife. And she was quite an attractive doll too which would make it easier to practise on.

I wasn't going to tell my wife about Candice. After all Mave's was a class for men and it might seem unfair to tell everyone, and also I wasn't sure what she'd say. I was going to buy a doll the following Saturday, but I had to think up an excuse as to why I was going out for the day so I told my wife I was going to one of the museums to look at the statues.

I'd had to get the instructions from Mave where to go to buy the doll. London is huge and very busy and it took a while figuring out where to get off the Tube and which direction to go from there. And looking at statues doesn't take all day so I needed to keep an eye on my watch. The Tube was very busy. I was thinking it would be a strange thing to be travelling on the Tube carrying a doll like Candice so I'd brought a holdall to put it in.

I had to get off at Tottenham Court Road station. I'd written that down at Mave's. From there it was about a ten minute walk to the area where I'd likely be able to buy a doll.

I knew it was the right shop because there was a woman's name above the door, that's what Mave had said. And there were statues of women in the window with virtually nothing on, mostly red and black garters and nightgowns.

Inside the shop was a bit fancy-looking with purple walls. Men and women were browsing the shelves, talking quietly, occasionally pointing things out to each other. Some of the things seemed quite rude. I went to the counter because I couldn't see any of the dolls on display – just undergarments and lines of plastic prong-looking things in cellophane packets.

The woman behind the counter was a nice-looking lady with long black hair wearing lots of make-up. She smiled and I told her I wanted to buy a plastic doll that you blow up. She continued to smile and called across to her assistant, another young lady but with a much paler face. She said something in a language I didn't understand. I thought they might be Russian. The woman left the counter a moment and returned soon carrying a pile of plastic packets.

She was very helpful which was nice. Had it been one of the shops where I live the woman serving would probably have scowled and looked disapproving.

The serial number from Mave's was different from the ones in the shop but she said it wouldn't matter, they were all much the same and all had fully operational parts. I wasn't entirely sure what she meant but she pointed at the picture on the packet, indicating its mouth – an oval shape that looked like a small plug-hole. I had the feeling the woman might not speak very good English. I don't know why she was pointing at its mouth, I wasn't planning to do much talking. I explained that I wanted to practise on it so I could satisfy my wife. When I told the woman this she smiled again and said something about the doll's privates which I didn't quite follow, but overall there didn't seem to be much difference between this one and Candice back at Mave's so I said I'd take it and she wrapped it up in a bag and said I could get a magazine for free, but when she pointed at them they were a bit rude so I said no. She then said 'enjoy' and gave me my change. So I said thankyou and left the shop. I forgot to ask about blowing the doll up but I guessed it would be like a bicycle tyre.

I decided to keep the doll in the bag on the train rather than getting it out to read the instructions because it was a bit crowded on the train and there wouldn't have been much room.

When I got home I needed somewhere to keep Candice. I couldn't keep her in the bedroom because my wife might find her, and I thought it best she didn't. So I put her in the bottom of the wardrobe in the spare room. Another problem was going to be having the chance to practise on her. I'd kept the booklet from Mave's in the drawer by the bed.

The night I went to Mave's my wife asked about it and I told her it had been very interesting. Lying on her side with her head propped on her elbow, she asked me if I'd learnt anything. She was speaking in a quiet voice, a bit like a child. I was thinking maybe she was feeling a bit guilty about telling me she wasn't satisfied. I said I'd learnt some things and she shuffled on the duvet and said 'what?' I thought it best not to tell her about the doll because she was a woman and it was a class for men and Mave might not like me telling her the details.

When Tuesday came we made love again and I tried to remember parts of the diagram Mave had pinned on the wall, but it wasn't easy having my wife underneath me *and* trying to remember what was on a diagram and I'd need a fair bit of practice to get it right. I wondered about getting the booklet out of the drawer but I had the feeling my wife might not like that idea, so I left it where it was and tried to remember bits. Afterwards I asked if she'd been anywhere nearer being satisfied and she said 'no, not really'. And then she rolled on her side and went to sleep or pretended to go to sleep.

I smoked a cigarette and thought about what she had said, and about Candice waiting in the foot of the cupboard in the spare room. I hadn't even opened the packet and read the instructions yet. But tomorrow was Wednesday. There was no 'Mave's this week and my wife would be going to her yoga class and then she'd be going for a drink with her friends from the class. While she was doing that I'd practise on Candice in the spare room. Feeling a bit better about soon being able to satisfy my wife, I stubbed the cigarette out and tried to get to sleep. Eventually I managed to nod off.

When my wife set off for her yoga class she asked me if I was going to be alright. She always asks me this, and I always say yes. I watched and waited till the car disappeared round the corner before I went up to the spare room and took Candice out of the wardrobe.

I'd been wise enough to buy a bicycle pump in town. He said it would fit all tyres and all inflatables. When I asked if it would fit on a plastic doll he stopped and thought about it for a minute, and then said it probably would, using a different valve. Which proved to be correct. It took a while blowing her up but eventually I managed it. I laid her on the bed and got undressed.

This Candice, like the one at Mave's, wasn't at all unattractive. She looked a bit like child's doll only huge with plastic blonde hair and big eyes and stiff arms and legs that looked a bit like sausage balloons but were quite shapely too which I think made them better-looking. She had breasts too which were small and jutted up like two plastic tea-cups topped with jelly-tots. And her mouth was wide open as if she was about to scream. She didn't close her mouth because she couldn't. It was funny seeing her mouth open like that. I kept expecting her to speak; to say something like 'Hello my name's Candice...' or something like that. Then it occurred to me that her mouth was open to kiss; like some people kiss – with their mouths open, which I thought was quite a good idea though it might seem a bit strange at first.

Once I'd taken my clothes off I picked up the instructions, but they didn't say much other than *Made in China* and how to blow it up. So I made my own investigation. There wasn't a great deal to see and some of the bits on Mave's diagram had been left out. But the rest of it was there and for a few minutes I read the booklet and investigated Candice's privates a bit closer. Of course, Candice didn't stir or move at all and I got to thinking whether my wife would move or stir if I was to do that sort of thing to her. Maybe I could ask her but it isn't always easy to talk about this sort of thing with your wife. It took a while getting ready to practise on Candice because although she was attractive, and looked like a *woman*, she was still plastic and a bit stiff like one of those air-beds at the sea-side. But she was pretty and I said her name her name a few times, not because I wanted her to answer me back but because it just seemed like the right thing to do, and that seemed to help.

At first it seemed a bit funny being inside a plastic doll but I could see Mave's point about bettering oneself and educating oneself to become a 'skilled lover' though I'm not quite sure what she meant by that; I know what the 'words' mean but not what *she* meant. Anyway I remember Mave saying something along the lines of 'timing our thrusts'. It was in the booklet along with the bits before starting to thrust; all on pages two and three. So I tried to time my thrusts counting to five each time and then, maybe because of all the counting, my arms started to ache and I had an idea not to support my weight on my elbows, but to lie on top of Candice, which I did. In a way it seemed strange lying on top of her, like I was being a bit unfair to my wife, but then I knew that was being silly because it wasn't with another woman, it was a doll, and I was only practising so I could satisfy my wife when we made love, which was the whole idea. So, lying on top of Candice, I timed my thrusts a little quicker, counting to three instead of five and then – rather suddenly and without really thinking about it – I kissed Candice on the lips, or mouth to be exact.

I hadn't planned to kiss her, it just happened. It seemed a natural thing to do with her lying under me with her mouth open wide, and me lying on top of her. Also, I thought that if you didn't kiss her what was the point in making her with her mouth wide open; it would feel a little bit like I was letting her down.

It was funny kissing her with her being plastic, a bit like kissing a rubber glove, but having her mouth open did make it easy and I was thinking that after a while, with a bit more thrusting and kissing, I might be able to satisfy my wife. For a moment I thought about the man behind me in the queue at Mave's, saying he wouldn't have any trouble satisfying the doll. It got me to looking into Candice's face, wondering, if she could speak, whether she'd say she was being satisfied, or like my wife – tell me she wasn't. It made me thrust a bit harder and again, without really thinking about it, I kissed her long and hard, and at one point, my tongue went in her mouth – though, like before, I hadn't really planned to do it.

After I had finished practising on Candice I smoked a cigarette, although I had to keep an eye on my watch; I didn't want my wife to come home whilst I was practising on Candice. Oddly, I had the idea of the whole thing being a big surprise – like a surprise party: I'm secretly practising on Candice in the spare room – then, later, get into bed to satisfy my wife when we make love. The cigarette got me thinking about practice-makes-perfect and that it might not be too long before I was able to satisfy my wife and stop her needing to look elsewhere to get satisfied. And, I quite liked Candice. She was nice-looking with big eyes and slightly rosy cheeks and blonde hair. And, although she was plastic, she was actually prettier than my wife, not that it's the same with my wife being a woman, but if Candice could help me satisfy her so much the better. Then, a peculiar thing: I got to thinking whether *I'd* been satisfied practising on Candice, and I couldn't answer that question. Maybe I had, and maybe I hadn't, and maybe it didn't really matter anyway.

As I stubbed the cigarette out I was thinking about the woman who served me in the shop; thinking whether she liked to be satisfied. Probably she did. I think women who work in shops like that like to get satisfied a lot, though I thought she might be Russian, and you can never be sure how they think about these things in Russia.

My wife came home about an hour later but I'd put Candice back in wardrobe long before that.

I'd been wondering about whether to try satisfying my wife the next time we were due to make love or whether to wait a while. But she had a headache so we cancelled it anyway, which was probably not a bad thing. As I smoked my cigarette I was wondering if she really had a headache or if she'd just said it, thinking a few more sessions at Mave's would be necessary before I could satisfy her. But then I remembered about 'trust', and that it was maybe as important as being satisfied and that, if push came to shove, I could ask her. But it didn't seem the right thing to do, and it isn't easy to ask your wife these sorts of questions – particularly if she *has* got a headache.

As I watched the cigarette smoke disappear into the patterns in the ceiling, I found myself thinking about Candice. It was strange to think about her wrapped in her cellophane packet in the wardrobe in the spare room. And then my wife lying next to me in bed. I thought briefly about Candice lying next to me in bed, but only briefly. It would be better to practise on her in the spare room.

Oddly, when the next opportunity came, not only was I thinking it would be a good idea to have another practice session on Candice, but I was quite looking forward to it. Before the first time I had wondered about being able to do it with her, but it had been okay: picturing Mave's diagram and seeing Candice blown-up for the first time had helped. This time I'd decided to try varying the speed of my thrusts and Candice wouldn't mind either way because she was a doll.

After I'd kissed my wife goodbye I waited a while before I went to the spare room to get Candice out of the packet. Whilst I was blowing her up I watched the way the plastic breasts slowly came to life like two pink mice rising from their sleep, stiffening to small peaks with red tips. I gave both a squeeze which was quite amusing and flicked the tips with my finger and then flicked her lips which – as ever – were wide open.

It was about five minutes after I'd started with the booklet open at page five above Candice's head, that I heard the door slam and footsteps on the stairs. I stopped looking at the booklet and panicked. When you panic you don't really know what to do. It's strange when you know there's nothing you *can* do. I knew it was my wife because of the way the door had slammed. Who else could it be?

All I can remember is pressing flat into Candice and closing my eyes as, moments later, the door opened and my wife saw us.

I heard her scream. And pressed into Candice because I had never heard my wife scream like that before and I didn't want to hear her and didn't know what else to do. Plus, I didn't want to look up at that moment because it might not be the best time to look at her, and she might not want me to. My wife didn't stay in the room long, only a few seconds and then I heard her stamping along the landing to our bedroom. I looked at Candice's open mouth and it looked like she was going to say something, that things were likely going to be a bit different now that my wife knew about her, but neither of us said a word. Instead I got off Candice and got dressed. Then I put her back in the polythene packet and put her back in the wardrobe.

I was thinking it might not be easy telling my wife about Candice and explaining it to her, and I was right.

It was unfortunate that she'd caught me practising on her because so far things had been going quite well. But it isn't always easy to explain these things to your wife. And, in any case, I wasn't sure she would listen. She was lying on the bed on her side as if she was asleep, but I knew she wasn't asleep, she was just pretending, and she was weeping. I wasn't sure whether it was best to stand and watch or go and sit next to her and try to explain that I'd been practising on Candice or whether to go downstairs and smoke a cigarette.

I decided to stay. I didn't like the idea of her lying on the bed crying and me sitting downstairs smoking a cigarette. Also it occurred to me that though it was unfortunate she'd caught me practising on Candice it needn't matter too much because she was a doll and my wife was a woman, and there was a difference. But all I could hear were sobbing sounds directed into the pillow as if she was trying to blot out everything around her, which in a way I could understand because she might have thought there was something going on between me and Candice.

I decided to sit on the edge of the bed. I toyed with putting my arm on her shoulder, which seemed the best thing to do, but she pulled her shoulder away and clenched her fingers clenched into fists that she pressed hard into the mattress. I tried telling her – partly to stop her crying and partly because I thought she ought to know – that I wasn't having a relationship with Candice, that I was only practising and I'd had the booklet open at page four, which proves it, but she wept again and curled herself away from me.

I could understand her crying because I knew what she was likely thinking: like me if I'd thought she was looking elsewhere to be satisfied. But it was unfortunate because it wasn't like that. For a spell neither of us spoke. It was like there was nothing you could think of saying that would likely help, so it's best not to say anything. It didn't seem the moment to tell her that with luck I'd soon be able to satisfy her. I didn't put my hand back on her shoulder; instead I asked if she wanted a cup of tea because a cup of tea can sometimes stop your wife crying.

But just as I was about to ask her, she raised her head from the pillow and looked me in the eye. It was the first time she'd looked me in the eye since she'd come home and

I guessed she was about to say something. What she asked was a strange question.

She asked me if the doll – though she didn't say 'doll' she said *thing* in a really angry way like she hated saying the word, that I'd been sleeping with – had a name. She was crying as she spoke and I couldn't really work out why she'd asked me. But as she had asked and she was upset about finding me with Candice, I thought I may as well tell her, though I felt 'sleeping with her' wasn't right because neither of us had slept and it wasn't like that.

When I told her the doll was called Candice she collapsed back into the pillow and started crying again, clenching her fists. I didn't like to see her crying and clenching her fists; it was only a name; it could have been any name. I couldn't see what was so upsetting about her name. It wasn't *her* name and neither of us knew anyone called Candice in real life.

It was difficult to know what to say or do for the best. It's always difficult to talk about these things to your wife.

The lamp at the side of the bed threw reflections across the duvet and she was suddenly looking very pale, her eyes red from crying. I wasn't sure she wanted to talk. There didn't seem much more to say at that moment. I'd explained why I'd bought Candice, that I was just practising, and for a while my wife stopped crying and stared with empty eyes at the bedside table. I knew that sometimes people needed a bit of space when they felt sad. I thought maybe my wife needed a bit of space. I went downstairs to smoke a cigarette.

In fact I smoked two cigarettes because smoking helps me think and I had quite a lot to think about. I thought about Candice folded up in the cupboard, oblivious to it all, and my wife curled up crying alone in bed. I looked at my watch. It was getting fairly late. I could put the television on for a bit but I don't really like watching television on my own. Or I could make a cup of tea and maybe take a cup upstairs to me wife though I wasn't sure whether she would drink it. The next thing I thought about was what effect all this would have on me being able to satisfy my wife when we made love. There were only eight pages altogether in the booklet and I was already on page five. It seemed unfortunate that it had been interrupted because my wife was thinking I was having an affair with Candice. But of course it wasn't really like that.

I wondered about sleeping on the sofa because when couple's fall out one of them sometimes sleeps on the sofa. But I didn't. I didn't really like the idea of sleeping on a sofa so I had half of another cigarette thinking, rather oddly, that my wife should be pleased I'd smoked it downstairs instead of in the bedroom where it tends to linger. I also wondered if my wife was being a bit unfair because I'd only bought Candice to help me satisfy her, and in a way, she was the one who started it.

I turned off the light and went upstairs. My wife was still lying on her side. She was either asleep or pretending to be asleep. I wasn't sure which, but thought she might be pretending because she'd been crying and there were no breathing noises. I faced the opposite direction and tried to get tired by thinking about things. I had a weird thought about whether Wilton Forelock ever practised satisfying his wife on a plastic doll. Soon after that, I fell asleep.

When I woke there was a shuffling sound and at first I didn't know what it was. Then I sat up and saw my wife putting things in a bag. When I sat up more, she looked me in the eye and told me she was going. I asked where she was going but she didn't answer. Maybe she didn't know or didn't want me to know. I asked her if she was going because of Candice. She didn't answer that either. She just put stuff in her case more quickly and closed the case. Only later, she said it was a stupid question. Maybe she was right.

At first I thought it was unfair that she was going like that because I didn't know where she was going or when she'd be back. And if it was because of Candice I'd told her I was only practising on her. I didn't want my wife to go. For one thing most of the time I did love her. I wondered whether to tell her this but decided not to. I wasn't sure if she'd listen or what she'd say.

Before she left, she stood a moment at the door. Her eyes were still red and her hair was looking a bit bedraggled. She didn't say anything at first, and then just said 'goodbye'. I didn't know what to say, so I said she didn't have to go, because it was all I could think of saying. But she said she did, and then took hold of the case and went outside. I didn't know whether she'd ordered a cab to take her where she was going, but I wasn't really thinking about that. I was only thinking that my wife was going, and I wasn't going anywhere and it had all been a bit unfortunate, and mainly – thinking about it – that it mattered that she wasn't satisfied when we made love.

I would have told her she could come back any time she wanted. But before I'd had a chance to say it, the door closed and she was gone.

After she had gone I mooched around for a while doing one thing and then another, and ending up doing nothing. It's a strange thing when your wife walks out and you're not sure if, or when, she's coming back. It gets you thinking. I smoked two cigarettes and looked at the picture on the wall where a child is crying because the family's dog has broken her doll. The girl looked sad and I understood why, if the doll had been special. Then I thought that my wife had been crying because of a doll too, but it wasn't the same because Candice wasn't broken, she was in a packet in the spare room. Then I got to thinking about where my wife might have gone and what she might be doing. I couldn't answer either question so I put the cigarette out and got out of my chair.

I made two cups of tea and ate a blueberry muffin whilst it was still fresh because I don't like them when they aren't fresh. And then I looked at my watch. I'd been looking at my watch a lot since my wife left.

I toyed with going for a walk to pass the time, and that's what I did. I didn't expect to meet anyone I know because I don't know very many people and meeting people in town isn't really a good idea because I can never think of things to say. And it's mostly my wife's friends. If I met one and she said 'How's your wife?' I wouldn't know what to say. I could tell her she'd left because of Candice but I'm not sure it would be a good idea. Plus, I was thinking she might come back soon. She might just have gone for a bus ride or a walk, which meant she wouldn't really have 'left'. Or maybe she'd gone to see her mother because wives sometimes go to see their mothers when they're upset. And then she'd come back and empty the case and say she just needed a bit of space, which is another thing people say when they're upset.

But at half past five she still hadn't come back, which was unfortunate as it was getting near tea-time and I'd end up making tea just for myself. I couldn't decide what to have. In the end I had boiled potatoes and beans with sausages in the tin. As I was eating it I was wondering what my wife was eating for tea and where she was. I wondered if she might phone later and tell me just in case I was thinking about it, but she didn't phone.

And then I was wondering if she was alone, or if she was with someone else, maybe a man who she thought might be able to satisfy her. Later I looked at my watch. The tv was on but I don't like watching tv on my own.

It was watching tv that made me decide to get Candice out of the cupboard. I don't really know why because – thinking about it – If I hadn't bought Candice my wife wouldn't have gone. So, in a way, you could blame Candice. But Candice was a plastic doll so it seemed a bit unfair to blame her; it wasn't really her fault, so there was no real need for her to be stuck in the wardrobe, particularly now my wife had gone.

So I got her out and blew her up and sat her next to me on the sofa. In a way it seemed a strange thing to be doing: sitting on the sofa next to a plastic doll. She looked the same as last time – the same big eyes and plastic blonde hair and big oval mouth looking, on this occasion, like it might be laughing; maybe laughing at the tv screen flashing away in the corner or at the fact that my wife had gone. I could look at her quite a few times with my wife not being there and she was quite a pretty doll. Prettier than a lot of women you see and prettier than my wife too. Though that doesn't necessarily mean anything because you don't have to be pretty. A lot of people you see are plain and ordinary-looking, and some are ugly, but they get by okay.

But looking at Candice got me thinking about my wife. And though she was prettier, she was a doll, not a woman, and there's a big difference. And I was wondering where my wife might be and who she might be with, and I don't think I'd be wondering that if it was Candice who'd walked out.

I looked at my watch a few more times and at the phone, wondering if it would ring. But it didn't, which was a shame. I would have quite liked it to ring and my wife tell me where she was and when she was coming back. It was around that time that I made a cup of hot-chocolate and ate two biscuits.

When I came back from the kitchen I looked at Candice and she hadn't moved an inch; she never did. I got to imagining it was because she was happy and had nowhere to go, even if she was only a doll. And naked, which was a bit odd, sitting there naked with her legs jutting out from the sofa, but with a smile on her face. I wondered whether to get a cardigan to put on her. My wife had several in the wardrobe, but I didn't because it would have been a bit of a strange thing to do, and in some ways it didn't really matter if she was undressed or not, being a plastic doll.

Which got me thinking about my wife again. It was unfortunate the way things had turned out, and on account of her yoga being cancelled. I felt it was all a bit unfair too: that maybe it shouldn't matter as much as this that she wasn't being satisfied when we made love, leaving the house and taking stuff with her in a case. And I got to thinking it wasn't necessarily my fault. But whether it was my fault or nor didn't really seem to matter, thinking who's to blame doesn't always help. But later, towards the end of the evening I felt sorry that my wife had gone. It seemed odd with her not being there. I didn't think about where she might be or who she might be with because I didn't want to, it would just make it seem more unfortunate that she had gone.

Instead I looked at Candice. She'd been sitting there a while now, just minding her own business and watching television. It was very late now and my wife obviously wasn't going to come back today. Maybe she'd be back tomorrow; you can never tell.

I turned the tv off and the lights off and checked the cooker. I don't know why I checked the cooker but I always do that. I tucked Candice under my arm and went upstairs.

It seemed a bit strange putting Candice next to me in bed. So far we'd only been together in the spare-room. The light from outside drifted in through the window and fell across her face, giving her the look of a child-ghost. Even in the dark you could see her small breasts jutting up like tiny blancmanges. Without thinking about it I gave them both a squeeze. Then lit a cigarette and started to think about my wife. One thing was it wouldn't matter how many cigarettes I smoked in bed because it wouldn't bother Candice whether the smoke lingered or not. Later I stubbed the cigarette out and turned to her.

I didn't think much more about my wife because I preferred not to, though I did wonder about what she might say about Candice lying in her place in bed. She probably wouldn't like that very much. But then she was the one who'd gone, and if she'd stayed Candice would have been in her packet in the wardrobe next door instead of in bed with me.

On this occasion I didn't bother with the booklet, I made love to Candice without it. The booklet didn't seem to matter so much with my wife not being here. It seemed best just to do whatever came natural: sometimes thrusting a bit quicker, sometimes a bit slower. And then – when the time seemed right – kissing her: a deep kiss, using my tongue. I was thinking what Mave would say about me doing that, but I don't think she'd say it was a bad thing to do. And Candice certainly didn't mind.

Timing my thrusts, I got to thinking...If Candice could speak, would she say she was being satisfied, or that I needed to practise a bit more yet. And then I realised I'd never know, and maybe it was a good thing not to know. Then I got to thinking whether I was satisfied, making love to Candice, but I still couldn't answer that question; most of the time I'm neither satisfied nor unsatisfied when I make love; I do it, and then smoke a cigarette. Maybe in some ways I was, and in some ways, I wasn't. And in some ways it didn't seem to matter anyway.

As I reached for a cigarette Candice was staring at the pattern in the ceiling. She got me thinking about 'trust' which with her would never be an issue. She was in bed with me because my wife didn't trust me, which was unfortunate. Maybe 'trust' isn't as easy – or as important – as some people think. I don't really know.

Seeing Candice open-mouthed next to me made me stub the cigarette out and reach across. I kissed her first this time, before anything else – a long kiss where my tongue was in her mouth for quite a long time whilst I reached down to fondle one of her breasts. The kiss lasted a long time, which didn't matter because we had a lot of time – all night long if we wanted. My wife wouldn't be back tonight, that was for sure; maybe not tomorrow either – or the day after. I wondered about getting the booklet out of the drawer, but wasn't sure I'd need it.

Candice was still staring at the ceiling. I breathed her name a few times and proceeded to the next step.

Post-script:
It was about a week later that my wife said she wasn't coming back, though she didn't say it, she left a message on the answer-phone. Maybe she left a message so we wouldn't have to talk about it, which, in some ways, wasn't a bad idea; I don't like talking on the phone because I can never think what to say. She just said she wasn't coming back and she hoped I'd be all right. Maybe she said this because she was the

one who'd left. She didn't say where she was or who she was with. She probably didn't say because she didn't want me to know. Maybe she'll come back some time, I don't know. To answer her question...I'm okay.

I have got used to cooking food and it is very quiet with my wife not being here. Candice is here but of course she doesn't say anything. Sometimes we sit together and watch television. I haven't gone back to Mave's since my wife has left.

I sometimes ask myself whether she left because she wasn't being satisfied, or because of Candice. I think it was probably because of Candice but you can't be sure, and you can't blame Candice; she's a plastic doll and it isn't her fault.

I suppose it still comes down to 'trust'. I sometimes mention it to Candice. I know she doesn't say anything because she can't, but I sometimes get the impression she's listening. Whether 'trust' is as important as being satisfied I don't know, I don't often think about it now.

The Coin

When John Bartholomew Little first came across the coin, he made little of it; it was just a *coin*. Not a regular coin – an item of recognised currency – more one of those commemorative – souvenir-type pieces – heavier and a little larger than your average coin. It was silver or at least silver coloured, and had maintained its almost pristine sharpness – virtually unblemished. He'd come across it whilst sorting through the pile of junk that had accumulated over the years in the top drawer of their bedroom dressing table – a task he'd been promising himself for some time and having arrived home from work a little earlier than usual, had finally had the opportunity to tackle.

The drawer turned out to be a monument to his past life: his old Walkman with its twisted, for some reason, pair, of headphones and a bevy of receipts and out-of-date envelopes and letters strewn into piles and bunches under wallets and dust.

He was about to make a decision on which bits to chuck, when he spotted something small and shiny at the bottom of the drawer, half concealed by a smattering of fluff. He took it in hand for further examination, rolling it a few times in his fingers and weighing it lightly in his hand, holding it to the light for a closer look. On one side was what looked like a castle or palace – two fine-looking spires heading off into the clouds through a finely decorated criss-cross pattern of lines. On the other side – a female figure, or girl to be exact; a beautiful girl: flailing hair and soft virginal features sweeping down to a kind of mermaid's tail that withered to a point near the edge. He brushed the coin against his shirt and examined it further, weighing both sides in

his palm, tossing it lightly from Castle-side to Girl-side. He had
no recollection of how it had come to be resting in the drawer
for what could quite likely have been years, but it was a nice
piece of workmanship; possibly some souvenir picked up on a
foreign market years ago.

He gave it a rub on his sleeve to embellish its shine and took
a moment to examine its surfaces more closely. Fine print
embossed round its circumference was impossible to decipher –
maybe a foreign language – possibly just miniscule scrawls. But
there was something about its shape and form – neat and snug,
heavier than a proper coin, but not to the point of weighing you
down – about the same size as one of those coffee-cup biscuits
they give you in a cafe.

He flicked it once; it spun lightly and easily. He popped
it on his left wrist – 'Girl side' up – he grinned and spun it a
few more times, going for a tally: best of three wins. Girl again.
The Girl wins! He was on the point of returning it to its place
in the drawer, when he had a sudden change of heart. After
turning it a few more times, he placed it in his rear trouser
pocket and went downstairs, where his wife was laying the
table for tea.

John Bartholomew's life was, and always had been,
painfully and inexorably dull. For as much of his fifty-five years
as he could remember little had happened that would warrant
so much as the space on an average-sized postcard. He woke
up, he got up, he went to work, he did hid work, he came home
from work. On his return home from work he would get his
shoes and his sandwiches ready for the morning, pour himself
a small whisky from the kitchen cupboard, eat his tea whilst his
wife sat opposite eating her tea. After which they would sit and
watch television for approximately four hours – they would
drink a cup of cocoa and then go to bed. Such were the lives
of Mr.J and Mrs. J Bartholomew: a set routine, undertaken
day in, day out, without fuss, without question and without
the urge to venture into any areas that might be set to disturb

it. They rarely listened to music, which seemed little more than a silly interruption of the airwaves. And rarely read, because books bored them, especially novels, which – though they never read any – were routinely unintelligible or tedious, quite often both. They watched television, or at least looked at it: the idea of something flickering away in front of them night after night –a reminder at least that time was passing – albeit at an alarmingly slow rate.

All of which brought him back to the coin, for there was no doubt that he was quite taken with his new find and vague ideas regarding to its future were already beginning to stir in his mind: ideas stemming first and foremost from the element of 'secrecy': that the coin was *his* and would remain *his* alone – safely concealed in his rear pocket. Even now, idling his time away in front of the box he could picture it nestling in his palm: the flowing locks, the tiny pin-prick eyes. It had that momentous feel to it. So much so that the urge to sneak another quick peep was soon quite overwhelming and he found him rising from his seat on the pretext of going to get a glass of milk from the fridge.

Once in the kitchen he withdrew the coin from his pocket.

It was just as it had been – mint clean and spankingly bright, certainly deserving more than to be merely schlepped around in his back pocket like some lucky-charm – the kind of thing schoolgirls have hanging off their pencil-cases. He turned it repeatedly 'Castle' side to 'Girl' side – the flowing hair, the pin-prick eyes as sharp as diamonds, the nymph-like expression set between near-invisible cheek bones. That would be the 'Heads' side, and the other side – the 'Castle' side – would be the 'Tails'. He gave it a few quick flourishes against his sleeve and then flicked it in the air, clamping it firmly on his left wrist. And as you do on these occasions, he guessed – 'Heads'. Correct. There was the girl, unmasked, beaming up at him through locks of flowing hair.

As he'd 'won' – guessed right – some kind of reward seemed to be in order, a kind of mini-treat. He looked round, waiting for some idea to spring to mind; a slice of his wife's Battenberg cake or an extra glug of whisky; but somehow it all seemed a bit tame; it needed something with a bit more whoomph than that – a bit risqué even. Which was how and when his wife came on the scene – and pretty much *where* the evening started....

It was during his next stint in front of the box that he found himself sneaking surreptitious glances at his wife, observing her in a way he had rarely done before. Fact was, he rarely gave her much thought. She was – after all – just his wife; sitting there – as was he: two fixed points in a never changing setting.

But on this occasion – he actually found himself observing her: the little acorn-head and tiny platinum bun of hair – both posed in perfect statuesque profile.

And as he sat ogling her, he could hear a small voice urging him to get over there and give her a kiss – not just a lightweight peck on the cheek, but a real mouth-to-mouth job, the kind of thing teenagers get up to at parties. As far as he could remember he'd never kissed her that way – not ever, but they were alone and it was night time, and they never went anywhere or did anything together...so why not?

But first he needed to get the go-ahead, the 'green-light' so to speak. He'd decided that the previous go would be the first of three: best-of-three in effect – that was another thing about the coin, apart from its appearance: 'Yes'/'No': Heads/Tails – nothing could be simpler.

It was as he was making his way back to the kitchen on the pretext of getting a glass of water that he decided that instead of having to guess the coin's outcome which could become a pain, the 'Girl' side, the *Heads* side, would be the 'green light' – the signal to go ahead; the 'Castle side – *Tails* would mean 'no' – idea aborted. That would make it simpler and far more practical.

He took the coin from his pocket and promptly flicked it, clamping it firmly on his wrist. There was the girl – beaming up at him from her gleaming metallic base.

Replacing the coin in his pocket, he stood a moment, brushing himself down before making his way back to the lounge.

She was still there – ready and waiting: the beehive bonnet, the acorn features, all perfectly posed against the backdrop of Laura-Ashley curtains.

Bracing himself, he strode briskly across the room so as to only temporarily interrupt her view of the tv set, and leaning across at an angle of some forty-five degrees, clamped his left arm round her neck. She'd barely had time to draw breath before their lips met, his tongue worming its way in and out of her mouth, from tonsils to teeth, and then back – five times in all, before withdrawing and restoring himself to full height.

For a moment his wife sat gagging and coughing profusely, spluttering into a napkin she kept handy on the side-table. After which, she appeared to freeze for a moment before recovering her senses sufficiently to ask what on earth he thought he was playing at.

Though the coin had said nothing about offering explanations, he felt obliged to come up with something.
'I love you,' he said, without blinking – looking himself in the mirror and straightening his collar. And managing to sound anything but convincing.

He watched as having attempted to regain her breath, she rose from her seat – his eye following her across the room. No way was he going to add anything or attempt to justify his actions beyond that. Rules were rules. He stood to one side to let her pass, taking a napkin from the arm of her chair and dabbing the last of her residue off his lips.

A minute or two later, she was back. Again he stood aside, trying to get his mind back into gear, watching her flop back into place, her eye by-passing him to fix itself on the tv screen. She reached for a chocolate biscuit, not realising that, in the heat of the moment, she'd sent the packet flying across the carpet. He knelt down and gathered the contents, replacing them one by one in the packet on the arm of the chair.

He continued to bide his time, checking for further signs of disturbance or ill-humour but there was little to report. Best to let things lie low for a while, maybe leave it till tomorrow.

Later – back in the kitchen, ditching the mugs in the sink, he leant against the window-sill, opened the window and gazed out.

It was a beautiful night: the silvery light creeping along the trees and rockeries. It almost made him want to get out there and be a part of it; to pose himself amongst the trees, looking manly and grand under the mantle of darkness. He briefly toyed with bringing the coin back into play but knew it was little more than a hangover from earlier and the reverberations that had followed. He'd best leave it for now.

A noise in the hallway caught his attention and he turned to see the lounge door closing. He assumed it was one of her regular toilet visits but a quick glance at his watch told him otherwise. He'd lost all track of time. His wife was stood in the hall. Then she turned and made her way to the stairs.

It was their habit for her to retire first and for him to follow shortly after. It was about fifteen minutes later, that, having completed his ablutions, he made his way along the landing, reaching the bedroom door where he stood a moment watching the moonlight drift across the corner of their dressing room table.

His wife was lying on the blanket, her head reclined, arms resting at her sides. She appeared to be staring at the ceiling – feigning ignorance of his presence perhaps or maybe highlighting the fact that her nightie had parted down one side.

He stopped in his tracks, finding himself staring in fascination at the sight of her exposed breasts – silvery clumps flopped on her chest like two bloated sparrows in the depths of sleep. For all her semi-nakedness, the words were sharp and as clear as glass. 'Well,' she said. 'Here I am.'

Her hand skimmed gently across the folds of skin, the words sylph-like – yet unavoidably croaky in their attempt to capture the appropriate mood.

'Well...you said you loved me.'

He watched another hand slide its way across the paunch of her stomach.

'It's alright. I understand, I'm your wife.'

Her head turned – facing him fully.

The nightie had splayed open. She hooked a knee and raised herself towards him.

'Well....?'

Again he found himself drawn to the moonlit cleavage; until – sensing the need for one of them to make a move – he turned and excused himself on the pretext of going to get a glass of water from the bathroom.

Fumbling in the semi-darkness, he made his way to a point where he couldn't be sure that there'd be enough light, but he'd try.

Taking the coin from his pocket, he weighed it once.... twice...his eye just about able to make out the castle-turrets and flowing locks of hair. And then he flipped it and clamped it firmly on his wrist. He peered through semi-closed fingers.

When he returned the nightie was back in place, the blanket and sheets refolded across her midriff. This time there was no acknowledgement of his arrival, her head remained pressed into the folds of the pillow.

As the coin found its way back into the drawer and he sat on the edge of the bed to remove his shoes and trousers, he looked over his shoulder; there were no signs of movement. He rested his head on the pillow and drew the bedclothes to the bridge of his neck. Behind him, his wife had already settled in her customary foetal-position, her eyes fixed on the window frame and its tiny squares of glass.

He looked at the green numerals displayed on the digital clock. In exactly one hour and twenty seven minutes another uneventful day would begin.

Games People Play

He detested parties, especially 'fancy dress'. They'd all be there; he could see them now: Long John Silver, The Belles Of St. Trinians, a fucking gorilla... the vicar with the protruding plastic teeth....Constance was going as a peasant wearing a shawl. She'd found a few bits of wood to tie to a stick for the broom and made a shawl out of bits of sacking she'd got cheap from a builder's yard. She wasn't going to wear the sacking until they got near to Mav's. She asked what he was going as. He said she'd find out.

The phone rang. It was Mel, checking out the plans and arrangements for the evening. She told her about the pub and the time and the arrangements they'd made with Bob and Carol, Paul and Roxanne. He took the tv mag and started browsing. She waited a moment and then turned to him. His face was buried in the tv pages.

'Mel's going as Bonnie, and Tom as Clyde: Bonnie and Clyde.'
She abandoned the phone and took her seat, extending her fingers for a quick resume on last night's mascara.

He started at Saturday, browsing his way down the two columns.

She turned an eye to the tv screen; it was sport.
'Bob and Pam'll be there tonight and Steve. Pam...as Florence Nightingale...and she hates hospitals.'

He turned to Sunday.

An impediment seemed to have lodged under one of her nails; she extended five fingers at arm's length for further examination. She looked across the room, her gaze stalling at the empty beer bottles lined on top of the sink, the top part of which was missing and then at the magazine shielding his face. She flicked a hand in the air, flexing and unflexing the five digits – a half-hearted plea for attention.

'I've been thinking about Australia.'

She held the other hand up for cursory inspection, tweaking each finger in turn.

'The place that Wally and Cynth were talking about – thirty miles from Sydney, on the coast. They said it's got a bit of garden – and there's facilities, shops and things nearby. And the place has just been done out. Remember...they said it'd had some work done in the kitchen and a new bathroom. And there's the car; Wally said his cousin was going to Adelaide first and would definitely be emigrating later this year.'

He turned to Tuesday.

'Think of it.....sun.....the beach...blue skies.....the coral reef...........koala bears.' She leant back in the chair, the images skipping tiny arpeggios across her mind.

He turned to Wednesday.

The afternoon was fading fast. She stared into the patio-window – the milky stains and tiny clumps of dead insects indelibly inked in the glass's surface looking almost surreal in the murky afternoon light. She extended the fingers on her right hand, noticing the few strains of last night's mascara still clinging in small patches near the half-moons.

She looked back across the room.

'John... you need to listen.'

Her voice remained flat – a deliberate effort to keep things on a level, so as not to shatter the air and ruin things. She looked across the room and did a quick count to three.

'I want us to make a go of it; a new start – a new life in Australia.'

She allowed the moment time to register before continuing, a little elaboration perhaps bringing a little more power to her elbow.

'It's a brilliant opportunity, one that might not come round again – lovely little place looking out across the ocean. I know there's an element a risk, there's bound to be. But I'm prepared to take a chance!'

She brushed a whisper of mascara from a nail and hung her head against the back of the sofa.

'John.....are you listening?'

He turned the page to Thursday.

She braced herself, her voice sinking to little more than a gentle whisper.

'And...I want you to be a part of it. To take a chance with me.'

She looked across, willing the magazine to drop, eager not to have her frustration go unnoticed.

'I know it's a big decision, but I want us to do something *big*! To be a bit adventurous – to do something different – to take a chance on something together for once in our lives.'

The magazine remained, stirring only as the page turned to Friday.

She sighed and lowered her head – brief contemplation of what she would likely concede had been an inevitability from the onset: the words that followed – pretty much the final straw...

'I just wanted to give you the chance that's all. Anyway, you might as well know – I'm going! I'm prepared to take a chance...and that's what I intend to do.'

She had at least found some success – it *had* all been markedly low-key. As if on cue – the magazine lowered to come to rest on the chair arm.

She watched as he sat – head bowed – hands clasped firmly in his lap almost as if he were about to say a small prayer. For a moment she thought he might be about to say something. But he didn't. He looked up briefly, then he rose to his feet.

She was only vaguely aware of him leaving the room and making his way along the landing to the bedroom.

She sighed, allowing both hands to drop to her lap.

The room was heavy with odours of cigarette smoke, dope and strains of joss-sticks. Constance hovered self-consciously by the door, donned in a long scraggy shawl and carrying a stick with bits of wood tied to it. She'd stuck some twigs in her hair and popped a few lipstick blotches on her cheeks beneath a few cat's whiskers of black mascara.

A few minutes later, he was back beside her, wearing a camouflaged army-type jacket and carrying a small shoulder bag. His face was covered in black smears and he wore a red bandana round his forehead. She watched him, wearing a puzzled expression. Nearby, Dracula was attempting to inflict love-bites on two naughty schoolgirls. He'd then tried it on with Cleopatra, but she reminded him she was his wife and told him to 'fuck off'.

Partly out of necessity in such a confined space – he pressed himself closer to Constance, pressing her up against the wall by the door. He looked down and smiled and she managed a kind of smile in return, though only through a still slightly puzzled expression.

He reached down and loosened the string of the shoulder bag he had kept at his side. Still grinning, he withdrew his hand and raised it to reveal a revolver.

She flinched as he raised it in the limited space between them.

"The Deer Hunter'...You know...Robert Di Niro.' His speech was decidedly slurred. There was no time for a response. He playfully raised the gun to her head and pulled the trigger. She flinched, dropping her drink, attempting, in a blind unfathomable panic, to turn away as it clicked next to her head. 'Russian Roulette...One shot is all it takes.....You take a chance....'

He levelled the barrel at his temple and pulled the trigger. 'See....'

The explosion sent some of his head and thick scarlet blood over Constance, Maid Marion and The Pope. He was vaguely aware of screams from 'The Belles Of St. Trinians' and Constance before most of him hit the floor.

He detested parties!